A PHARMACY OF LIES

A PHARMACY OF LIES

AN ANGELO BARSOTTI MYSTERY · BOOK 2

RYAN SPELL

Ryan Spell, LLC
Lake St. Louis, MO

Published in the United States by Ryan Spell, LLC, Lake St. Louis, Missouri.
First Edition

The story, all names, characters, and incidents portrayed in this production are fictitious. Any similarity to real persons, living or dead, places, buildings, and products is coincidental and not intended by the author.

Edited by Karen L. Tucker, CommaQueenEditing.com
Book design: Peggy Nehmen, n-kcreative.com

ISBN:
979-8-9874618-6-0 - paperback
979-8-9874618-4-6 - ebook
979-8-9874618-5-3 - hardback

Library of Congress Control Number: 2024915149

BIASC
FICTION / Mystery & Detective / Private Investigators
FICTION / Mystery & Detective / General
FICTION / Thrillers / Crime
FICTION / Crime

Dedicated to my wife, Dawn,
for being supportive on this journey
and for helping me pursue my dreams.

PROLOGUE

A LIGHT DUSTING OF snow covered the ground. It was just past dusk, so only the moon lit the sky. The footprints leading up to the house would be covered with new snow within an hour. He was happy with how his plan had worked so far. He knew she was home alone, and he was already at the house without anyone passing by.

He had been hired to kill the woman in the house and make it look like a robbery. He only knew her name was Lucy, and it was important she end up dead. He did not need to know any more information, just that she was the only one who was to be killed. No other casualties were permitted, or he would not be paid.

Her husband had left an hour ago. He rang the doorbell then swiftly but silently jogged to the back door. He knew the back door was always unlocked from his previous visits preparing for tonight. As she opened the front door, he quickly slipped into the house.

She looked around, even called out, "Hello?" before she shut the door. She just shook her head, a bewildered look on her face. She turned out all the lights and headed for bed. She never saw him coming.

As she walked into her bedroom, he shot her twice: once in the shoulder and then close range to the back of the head. He did not want it to look like a professional hit. These were his instructions.

He promptly proceeded to the next step—trashing the place. He opened every drawer in the bedroom and threw clothing everywhere. He also dumped her jewelry box, scattering it out all over the floor. He moved from room to room, ransacking everything he could. He was not to take anything except for money but make it clear he had been there. Taking money would at least make it appear to be a cash grab.

Everything was accomplished in thirty minutes, right as his watch timer went off. He exited out the back door and headed into the small, wooded area that backed up to a neighbor's house. He slid along the left side of the house, as he knew there were no security lights on that side. He quickly reached his car that was parked on the street that ran parallel to Lucy's.

He sat in his car for two hours when he finally heard the sirens. He started the car and drove by the house for a final look at the commotion he had caused.

CHAPTER 1

"WE NEED TO TALK…"

The clouds turned gray and thunder erupted, breaking my astonishment. I was snapped back to reality with Vanessa standing in front of me with a sad and fearful face. Her blue eyes seemed to have lost a touch of their sparkle.

"Vanesa…" I hugged her tightly. I couldn't even gather my thoughts enough to say more. My head was racing with a million questions. I wanted to ask all of them at once and just shake her until she told me every detail, but finally I settled on, "Are you OK?"

"Yes, I'm just scared. I've been running and hiding for too long, and I promised you that I would tell you everything when you finished with Helen's murder investigation. So, I'm here, but I still don't feel safe. Can we leave now?"

We walked to the car, where Lewis was waiting. As we ducked into the car, the floodgates opened, the rain crashing down hard against the metal of the car. We had narrowly missed getting soaked.

"Vanesa, I don't even want to let you out of my sight for fear that you won't be there when I turn around, but Lewis and I need to go to Helen's funeral reception. We'll take you to Lewis's penthouse, and he'll have extra security on guard." I looked at Lewis, who was nodding approval. "We will come back as soon as possible. Are you OK with that?"

"It's not ideal. I want to talk to you. I need to tell you what I know and why I am running. But I understand. You do everything with a purpose and see it through to the end. So, I know that you must close this chapter, and you need to go to the reception to do that. I'll rest and be waiting for you both when you get back."

When we pulled up to Lewis's building, Lewis took Vanesa up to his penthouse. I stayed in the car, knowing that if I went up, I wouldn't come back down. I wanted answers, and I have waited so long, but Vanesa was right. I do not do things halfway, and Helen deserved for us to finish what we started. Also, people were expecting us to be there, and I don't like to disappoint others.

I grew up in New York, but like I've said before, Lewis and I come from different pasts. My parents took care of my brother, Joseph, and me, and they did the best they could. We weren't exactly poor, but we were on the below average side of income. What I got most from my parents, though, were the values they instilled in me. They taught me to continue to work hard, do what you say you'll do, and trust in those close to you, and in the end, life will provide. Joseph and I both became good people with the desire to help others. I am, as you know, an investigator, and Joseph is a New York City firefighter. We help others in our own way, and both are on a mission to make the world we live in a better place, even if just in our small corner.

Lewis came back down and told me Vanesa was already asleep. We headed to Helen's funeral reception in silence, listening to the rain pelting the car and thinking of what would come next.

CHAPTER 2

HELEN'S RECEPTION WENT OFF as planned, and everyone was able to put closure to the whole situation. We heard many stories of how many clothes Helen had, her influence in the fashion industry, and what a good friend she'd been. It was nice to hear how well people spoke of Helen and see how close friends of hers were. We also heard disbelief from several friends that Craig had been involved in her murder.

Now, Lewis and I were standing out on the patio, as the rain had cleared up. The sun was peeking through the clouds, and the few rays were warm on my skin. Things could be heading in the right direction. Lewis said, "So, we'll talk to Vanesa when we get to my place. I would suggest starting delicately, Boss. She's been through a lot."

"I know, Lewis, thanks, but…" My phone buzzed with a text message. It was from my brother Joe.

My brother and I aren't close, but we aren't estranged either. We see each other at family gatherings, holidays, and the occasional meetup if something is going on. We don't communicate on a regular basis though. So, when I saw the text was from him and what the message was, I knew things were not headed in the direction I thought.

It read: *Angelo, I know it's been a while, but we need to talk.*

I wrote back: *When and where?*

"Sorry, Lewis, it's my brother, and he needs me. Can you take me there when this is over?"

"Got it, Boss."

▪ ▪ ▪

The rest of the reception went on without any more bombs being dropped on my life. Joe had asked for me to come to his home, and I told him that Lewis and I would be there as soon as the reception was over.

Joe is a firefighter; that's his life. He has been married once, and has a son, Logan, who is seven years old. The marriage didn't last long because Joe is dedicated to being a firefighter above anything else. Eventually, this was what broke his marriage. But even though he couldn't save his marriage, he is a great father when he has Logan.

Lewis and I headed for Joe's apartment. I knew we had to go right away because Joe never asks for help. Ever. Something must be terribly wrong.

CHAPTER 3

WHEN WE ARRIVED AT Joe's apartment building, he was outside pacing back and forth, clearly agitated. He saw us as we got out of the car. He rushed over, saying, "I'm not sure about this."

"Not sure about what, Joe? What's going on?" I asked, trying to calm him down with a soothing demeanor.

"Look, Angelo, I'm struggling with what to do here. It's way above my pay grade. I'm just a firefighter, nothing more. I'm not sure if I should even say anything at all."

Lewis stepped in. "Joe, why don't you start with telling us what's going on, and then continue further if you feel like it when you get through the first part?"

"OK. There have been some arson cases…well, what we all thought were arson cases. But then when we get the reports back, they were deemed accidental by the fire investigator."

"Joe," I said as I put my hand on his shoulder, again trying to calm him, "that's their job, right? They're the ones who determine what happened with the fire."

"No, Angelo, I mean yes, but there's no way the last two fires at research facilities were just accidental. The fires were huge, and…" Joe's voice trailed off as he searched the sky, as if looking for answers. He struggled with what to say next. I wasn't sure if it was because he didn't know what to say or didn't know if he should be saying it aloud.

I looked to Lewis for some help. He suggested, "Hey, Joe, why don't we grab a drink, maybe a beer or something, and we can just talk this through?"

Joe was still looking up but finally looked at me and asked, "Do you still work at McGinty's?"

"Of course, I do. Roy can't get rid of me! I'm the best bartender that has ever worked there!"

Joe shot Lewis a look, and they both doubled over in laughter. I stood in mock astonishment and said, "What? What are you both laughing at? It's the truth!"

Lewis, who had started to tear up from laughing so hard, said, "Yeah, you're the only bartender! And Roy only likes you because you saved his cookies in the second grade!"

Joe chimed in, "Yeah, let's head there, and we'll see what Roy thinks about your proclamation!"

We all piled into Lewis's car and headed for McGinty's. At least I was able to calm Joe down some, even if it were at my expense.

▪ ▪ ▪

We walked through the door at McGinty's. The crowd was light, as it was dinner time. The cops usually came after dinner with their families or when they got off the second shift. Roy shouted as soon as he spotted us, "Hey, everyone, the best bartender that has ever worked here just walked in!"

The laughter started all over again. Lewis must have sent Roy a message, and Roy never misses a chance to have a good laugh.

"OK, guys, I get it. Can we just get some beers, Roy?" I asked. I knew it was all good fun, but we needed to figure out what was going on with Joe.

We took a high-top table near the bar, and Roy brought us three beers in cold frosted mugs. Once he walked away, I said, "All right, Joe, what is it you're not telling us?"

"Fine. Let's start with the fact that we all believed it was arson. There was an accelerant at both fires. We know the smell of ethyl alcohol, and it was there."

"But you said that it was research facilities that burned down. Don't they use ethyl alcohol in those facilities?" Lewis asked.

"Let me get there, Lewis. Both facilities were research facilities. More specifically, they were pharmaceutical research facilities. And yes, they do use ethyl alcohol. But it was everywhere. We got there before the blaze erupted at the first one and went inside. The second we went in, the smell was overwhelming, like it was doused on every inch. We got the hell out of there because it was only a matter of minutes before the fire engulfed the building. We tried to control the fire, but the building was essentially a shell within a few hours. When we were interviewed by the fire investigator, we all told him what we smelled when we walked in, but he still ended up ruling it an accidental fire due to poor wiring. His explanation on the smell was that where we entered was near the storage area and that was why the smell was so strong."

I jumped in as he paused and asked, "Well, doesn't that explain it then? Why would he lie?"

"Angelo, I am a firefighter and have been doing this my entire adult life. I live and breathe this job. When I tell you the building was covered in ethyl alcohol, it wasn't just a storage area nearby, I promise. In the end, though, my captain told me to let it go, and I did. Then the next fire came, and it was exactly the same. Even the investigator's report was almost a copy of the first report. Also, there's something else about the second facility, Angelo."

I waited for him to go on, but again, he was struggling. So, I prodded him, "What is it, Joe?"

"The second facility was where Lucy worked."

We sat there in silence, the last sentence echoing through the room like I was in a cave. There's no way this was a coincidence.

CHAPTER 4

WE DROPPED JOE BACK off at his apartment. He said he would call us tomorrow. Now that he had gotten it off his chest, he said he needed to think about the next steps. Lewis and I don't know enough about fires or arson to do much until he gives us more, and we needed to get back to Vanesa.

On the ride back to Lewis's, he asked me, "What do you want to do, Boss?"

"I want to talk to Vanesa; I hope she's awake when we get back."

"That's great, Angelo, but I was asking about what Joe said. Do you think there's any connection with Lucy's murder and the research facilities burning down?"

"I haven't worked that out yet. But with Lucy's building being involved, I want Vanesa's take on it. Also, we don't know for sure that it was arson. I know Joe is smart and good at what he does, so I tend to believe him, but I need more facts first. Do you know anyone who could pull the fire investigator's reports for us from those two fires?"

"I'll get right on it. But since you brought up Vanesa, how are you going to handle her? You can't just go guns blazing and bombard her with questions."

"I know, Lewis, and I think I've been quite controlled so far. I want her to tell me in her own time, but with her history of running from something, and now this new information from Joe, we need to get some answers sooner rather than later."

▪ ▪ ▪

As we walked into Lewis's building, struck me once again that it was a sparkling masterpiece. The attendant said hello to me by name and sent us to the elevator. After ascending, the elevator opened to Lewis's penthouse. It was once two condos that he converted into a penthouse suite. Lewis asked his butler if Vanesa had been seen awake yet, and he said no.

Lewis went into the kitchen and came back out with a couple of beers. I said, "What do we do now?"

"We wait until morning."

"I'm not leaving. I want to know more as soon as possible."

"You're welcome to one of the guest rooms, Boss. You may want to head to bed soon. I have a feeling tomorrow is going to be a long day."

"It's definitely going to be hard to get to sleep tonight, but this beer should help," I said and then chugged the entire bottle.

"Angelo, I know that I'm not always the serious one, but listen to me. We will figure this out. I'll help you get the closure you need. We need to approach this whole situation delicately because there seems to be a lot of different parties involved, and we don't even know who the players are yet. Let's do our best to get some rest and start fresh tomorrow. I love you, buddy."

"Thanks, Lewis, I love you too. Good night."

CHAPTER 5

SLEEP DID NOT GO well. I tossed and turned all night, wondering what Vanesa would say and what more Joe had to say. *How could this all be tied together? Is it tied together?*

Despite the restless night, I still got up early because I wanted to be up when Vanesa got up. It was barely four in the morning, so I treaded lightly to the refrigerator to grab a bottle of water. I headed out to the terrace to take in the morning air.

New York at 4 a.m. on top of this building was amazing. This truly is the city that never sleeps because, even at that time, there was traffic, horns blaring and people yelling, and I loved every second of it. But I tuned all of those sounds out and just breathed. This helped me clear my head and get ready for the day.

Lewis's butler appeared and asked if I'd like some coffee. And I said sure. I hoped I didn't wake him up. But coffee was what I needed right then, as the air was chilly and I needed to wake up fully. He brought out a cup of steaming hot coffee and asked if I'd like anything else, and I told him this was perfect for now.

Out walked Vanesa, also carrying a cup of coffee. She approached me slowly, like she was unsure of herself. I said brightly, "Well, you're up early! How did you sleep?"

She smiled, her blue eyes sparkling in the sun that was just peaking over the horizon. She said, "Actually, I haven't slept like that in a long time. It was exactly what I needed. I felt safe here."

"You are safe here."

"I know that now, Angelo. But I haven't felt safe since the night we had dinner. It was such an amazing night and I'm sorry how it turned out in the end."

"You have nothing to be sorry about. Obviously, you had something to run from because they came to your parents' vacation home looking for you. Luckily Lewis found you first. But Vanesa…" I paused, not wanting to push her too fast, but I went through with it anyways, "what were you running from? You said it was the same people who murdered Lucy, and until that moment, I didn't even know she was killed for a reason. I just thought it was the wrong place, wrong time. Can you help me out? At least fill me in a little?"

"Yes, Angelo. That is why I came back. But it's a long story, and I'll need to go back to the beginning to give you the full picture of what is going on."

▪ ▪ ▪

"It started when I first met Lucy."

"You knew Lucy?!" I said with more volume than I meant to.

"Yes, Angelo, but let's save all the questions until I'm finished, or I may not be able to get through it all."

"Sure. Sorry."

"Actually, Mr. Touré met her first. He heard what she had to say and decided that I would be the right one for the case. When Lucy came to our law firm, she was looking for legal help to do with her job as a researcher for a pharmaceutical company. I want to let you know this is an ongoing case, so I need to leave some particulars out, but I'll do my best to tell you everything that I can.

"Well, in her research, she found that a certain drug would cause many problems for those who took it. She took her concerns to her bosses, and they said they would look into it. Instead, they released the drug, knowing full well what harm it could cause. Lucy didn't do anything at first, hoping that she was wrong and those above her knew what they were doing. Then people started dying or became extremely unwell. She tried one more time to talk to her superiors, but they just looked the other way again. This is when she came to us.

"Originally, she was wondering what she could legally do about the situation. She'd signed a non-disclosure agreement that prevented her from discussing anything that happened within the workplace, including any of her research. But there was a clause, way down in the fine print, where it states anything that could cause harm to others nullifies her non-disclosure agreement. Once we explained the process, we got the whole story.

"First, we walked her through the Whistle Blower Protection Act, or WPA for short. This law was put in place in 2014 to protect the person who whistle blows from retaliation from the company that they spoke out against. Essentially, they could not fire her or reduce her work or work conditions in any way. Then we began putting together a class action lawsuit against her company for the people hurt by the drug. She gave us all the particulars of the drug and what could happen.

"Then two weeks after we filed the lawsuit, and asking for people who were affected by the drug to come forward, Lucy was killed. She was the star witness, what the case hinged on. And I believe that is why she was murdered."

I sat there stunned. Lucy had never talked about any of this to me. She never even acted differently. I know now that she couldn't talk to me about any of this, but it doesn't make the news any easier to take. Vanesa just waited for me to respond. She knew it was a lot to take in and could tell it was the first time I had heard all this information.

I had realized we were still sitting outside, and the air was brisk. I suddenly had chills running throughout my body, and it wasn't from the breeze. I also noticed Lewis sitting nearby. I wondered how long he had been there. I had been so focused on Vanesa's words, my mind was oblivious to anything else.

Finally, I stood and said, "I have so many questions, but I need to digest this first. Lewis, can I borrow some gym clothes? I need to go for a run."

CHAPTER 6

WHEN I HAD GOTTEN back from my run, Lewis and Vanesa were having breakfast. The food smelled amazing, but I really wanted a shower first. Lewis asked if I wanted anything, and I replied I would take whatever he was having and proceeded to the bathroom to shower. I turned on the water, first listening to the constant pitter-patter. It calmed me down, and I jumped right in. I like cold showers, especially after a good hard run. It also erased my mind, at least for a few minutes, because all I could think about was the cold.

After getting dressed, I checked my phone for the first time today. There was a missed call and a text from Joe. The text simply said: *I'm ready.*

I didn't reply right away; instead, my head took me elsewhere. I was suddenly hit with a memory of Lucy. We were sitting at a coffee shop, and she was telling me about work. She said, "Angelo, there's some issues going on at work. I can't really talk about it, but I wanted you to know that I have some conflicts that I need to talk to a lawyer about. As soon as I can talk to you about it, I will, but for now, just be there for me. I know how you like to solve problems, but this one I need to do my way."

I was back in my room at Lewis's. I felt a sudden pang in my chest. She had told me about all of this, but I didn't remember until just now. Obviously, I wished I had asked more questions, but I trusted my wife. She was a strong woman, and much smarter than me. But what if I had pushed back, just this once?

I walked out to join Lewis and Vanesa for breakfast, pushing my thoughts to the back of my mind. I looked at Lewis and said, "Joe's ready."

Vanesa looked at both of us and asked, "Who's Joe?"

"Joe is my brother, and he has a case he wants us to look into. It may actually be tied to your case and Lucy. The long and the short of it is that two research facilities had fires. Officially, they were ruled accidental, but Joe believes otherwise. One of them was the building that Lucy worked at. But that's all we know so far. His text said he's ready, meaning he is ready to tell us more."

Vanesa got a little excited and said, "Well, what are we waiting for?"

"I already texted him back that we could meet up this afternoon, but I'm ready also. I need to ask you some questions first. I want to know more about Lucy and this case. Just let me eat and we can talk."

"OK, Angelo, but will you let me come along to meet Joe?"

"Let's talk about it after I eat whatever this is. What is this, Lewis?"

"It's soft-shell blue crab eggs benedict with roasted potatoes. It is one of my chef's specialties. You will love it!"

▪ ▪ ▪

Once again, Lewis was right. I loved every bite. As I finished, we all stood and went over to the oversized couches Lewis had in the living room. I settled in across from Vanesa, with Lewis on the other end of the couch. "OK, Vanesa, like I said, before we get into what Joe thinks, I need to ask you some things. I will try and not interrogate you, but know I am just trying to get a solid starting point. If at any point you feel uncomfortable, just say so and we can take a break. But, I promise, this will also be very uncomfortable for me."

"I understand, Angelo. I know this has probably been weighing on you for two years, and especially the last few months after I dropped that bomb on you, and I'm sorry about that. But I do really want to help, and I'll answer the best I can. Also, when I get back into the firm and talk things over with the partners, we can maybe figure out a way for you to get all the details as well. What do you want to ask?"

"First, why would someone kill Lucy over this?"

"Money…it's always money, Angelo. Even without the lawsuit, had they followed her advice to start trials over and fix the errors, it would have meant over hundreds of millions of dollars, if not billions, lost on revenue. It's a numbers game to them."

"But wouldn't they know that there was a possibility of this? Isn't that why they have researchers and trials?"

"I cannot answer fully for them, but from what I understand, she brought this to their attention after all trials had concluded and a release was already set for this drug. This is when the aftereffects were discovered by Lucy. She figured out what could happen if it went out for mass production. And she tried to stop it.

"To answer your other question, they have researchers to advise them, but at the end of the day, they make decisions based on their bottom line. They took the risk and decided it was worth it. Obviously, human life is not the major leading factor for them, including Lucy's."

"So, you believe that 'they' killed her to silence her? If so, why after two years are they after you now?"

"Well, I had reopened the class action lawsuit. Once Lucy was killed, we had to get the courts to order a continuance so we could try and gather more evidence of the case. Lucy was our main witness and main source of evidence. And since then, we have been gathering breadcrumbs that Lucy left behind for us. Once we had enough, we reopened the suit. I had just refiled the case when I figured out I was being followed. That was the night you and I had dinner together."

Getting a little agitated, I asked my next question, "So, if you know who killed Lucy and who is after you, why can't we just go to the authorities?"

After a sidelong glance at Lewis, Vanesa answered, "Angelo, these are powerful people. They have money and resources. They would not have any ties to them being involved with Lucy's murder, and I want to get them where it hurts the most—their pockets. If I simply tried to turn them in, I would very well end up just like…" her voice trailed off.

"Like Lucy, is what you were going to say," I said, but not harshly, more with compassion. "I get it, Vanesa, but how can we do anything about it then?"

"We need to pursue the lawsuit and find someone else who is as strong as Lucy was to come forward. At the same time, you and Lewis need to pursue an investigation into them and find a way to prove they killed Lucy."

"How can I do that if you won't even tell me who they are?" Again, I raised my voice more than I intended to.

"I have an idea, but like I said, I need to talk to the partners and get them to sign off on it. It shouldn't be a tough sell; just give me a little more time."

CHAPTER 7

LEWIS WENT WITH VANESA to her office, and he had one of his drivers take me to McGinty's. As soon as I walked into the bar, Roy started in on me, "Your shift doesn't start for another four hours! You're never early, so what are you doing here already?"

"Can't I have a beer with my brother in peace, Roy?"

"You came to the wrong place for peace!" Roy shouted as he laughed loudly with the few customers at the bar.

Ignoring the laughter, I walked behind the bar and said, "I guess I'll serve myself then!" as I grabbed two beers from the cooler.

"It's probably the most work you'll do all day!" Roy laughed again.

I found a table off to the side and waited for Joe to arrive. I heard Roy before I saw Joe, "And there's the better-looking Barsotti! How you doing, Joe?"

"I'm good, Roy. How are you?"

"I'll be better when your brother actually works, but you know I can handle it. Nice seeing you!"

Joe pulled up a chair next to me, leaned in, and said, "Hey, I forgot you work at a cop bar. Let's finish these beers and take a walk?"

I gave him a strange look, but I nodded and started to drink my beer. Joe nervously tapped the table and was slow to even take a sip. Finally, we were both done and stood to leave without one word between us. Roy noticed us as we were walking out and shouted, "I guess I'll just put those on your tab, Angelo?" He was laughing as he moved on to doing something else.

▪ ▪ ▪

Once we were outside, I said, "What was all that about?"

"Look, Angelo, I know what I've already told you seems crazy, but what I say next is next-level crazy. And what I have to say cannot be said in *that* bar."

I waited patiently for Joe to say more. He didn't need a push right then; he just needed to convince himself that he wanted to talk to me. So, we continued walking until he stopped and said, "I think the NYPD is involved in these arson cover-ups. Not the whole force, obviously but some."

"That's a big accusation, Joe. I'm guessing there's more because I know you wouldn't say this about your brothers in blue without some proof."

"In both fire investigations, our fire investigator, Nathan Grimble, was pulled off the case by the police's fire investigator. When I asked him why, he said he was told that the type of facilities and the sensitive information and documents inside made it a police matter."

"Isn't that an acceptable explanation?"

"I asked Grimble the same question, and he said no, it has never happened before like that. Usually, the police only get involved if it has already been determined to be arson or if a murder has occurred. And since he hadn't made any determination officially, it should have still been his case. So, when I pressed him further, he clammed up and told me to 'Just let it go.'"

"Still, Joe, that's a big leap. How can you be so sure this is a cover-up?"

"There's more, Angelo. At both fires, the sprinkler systems had been turned off. When we arrived at each facility, there was no fire suppressant or water coming out of the system. I've read both reports that the police investigator wrote up. They both say accidental from poor wiring, and there is no mention of accelerants or that the sprinklers malfunctioned. These are major items left out of a report. So, either the police are covering something up or committing major insurance fraud."

"OK, I believe you, but what do you want me to do?"

"I want you to investigate the NYPD. Someone needs to figure out why they are doing this, and I thought you may want to know as well, since one of the buildings was where Lucy worked.

"And Angelo, before you decide, I need to tell you one more thing. This was the real reason I was struggling to tell you any of this. The night Lucy was killed, I was on duty at the firehouse. We heard the call go out, but it wasn't inside city limits, so it wasn't our call. But I recognized the address immediately. My commander allowed me to go to the scene, but only as a concerned citizen, not as a firefighter. When I showed up to your house, you were pretty distraught… Do you even remember me being there?"

"Of course, I do. That night replays in my head all the time."

"OK, do you remember who the police officers were that you talked to?"

"Not really, but it was the NYPD. Why?"

"Angelo, I was told I couldn't be there as an official firefighter because it was outside city limits, so what were the NYPD doing there? It should have been the local authorities from your county. It never really bothered me until these arson cases came up and then the probable cover-up. And they both involve Lucy…."

I think he said more, but when he said, "They both involve Lucy," my mind went blank. The next thing I know, Joe was slapping me and asking if I was OK. He said that I had fainted and was lucky I hadn't cracked my head open. No, my head didn't crack, but it had just exploded a little.

CHAPTER 8

WE HEADED BACK TO my apartment. I needed to clear my head, obviously, so we walked in silence. Joe knew when to give me space and when to push, so he wordlessly strolled beside me. I needed to go inside and change for work, but when we got to the front of my building, Vanesa and Lewis were waiting there.

"Are you OK, Angelo?" Vanesa asked.

I glanced wearily at Joe, figuring he had texted Lewis about me fainting, and then answered Vanesa, "Yes, I'm good, but we all need to compare notes. Right now, though, I need to get changed and get to the bar."

"Angelo, you just fainted. Are you sure you're good to work?" Vanesa asked worriedly.

"I think Joe may have exaggerated a bit," I shot Joe another look. "I just lost my balance while we were talking, no big deal. Right now, I do need to work. All this talk has been flooding my brain with memories and things I may have missed before. So, a night at the bar is just what I need right now. I hope you received good news at the law firm, but can we all meet up tomorrow to move forward with everything?"

Lewis is good at reading me and knew what I needed at this moment. He replied, "Sounds good, Angelo. You go to your bar where you're regarded as the best bartender ever and then get some rest. We do have a lot to talk about, but it can wait. Do you two want to grab dinner? My treat!"

Joe and Vanesa both agreed, but Vanesa gave me one more look just to make sure I was truly OK. I just nodded, letting her know I was without any verbal communication.

■　■　■

As I showered and got ready to go to the bar, my mind replayed that fateful night. I still blocked the memory of seeing Lucy in the bedroom, but I saw images of the police. I remembered an officer asking me questions, going through where I had been, who would do this, and so on.

Wait! I had to do that twice. Right after the officer finished questioning me, another officer approached. He said, "I know you just went through this, but I need to ask it all again, for our records." I was in such a state of shock and sadness that it didn't occur to me that I had originally talked to the county police, but the second officer was from the NYPD. What had he said next? What was his name? Why can't I remember? This is my profession.

I stood there looking in the mirror, disgusted that I couldn't remember something so important. I began questioning myself and what I claimed to be. And then I thought back to Lucy and how she would leave words of encouragement for me in the mirror. Any morning that she would shower before me, she would always write something on the mirror so that when it steamed up again, and I got out of the shower, I would see it. She would write things like LOVE, BELIEVE, and TOGETHER. She wrote many other words, but these were my favorites. Recalling this treasured memory calmed me.

▪ ▪ ▪

I spent so much time getting ready and thinking, I ended up being late to the bar. And Roy never lets me off the hook for it. I don't ever really get in trouble, but he gives me a good ribbing. Tonight was no different because when I walked in, he said, "You have got to be the only guy to show up four hours early and then still end up late for your shift!"

I usually don't respond because, if I do, he only gets worse. I just let him have his fun at my expense; in the end, I deserved it. Although if I showed up on time, he would find something else to poke fun at me for, so, oh well. Just Roy being Roy, and I love him for it. Keeps me on my toes. And I could use a good laugh tonight.

The bar was busy enough to keep my mind focused on bartending. It was what I was longing for after the day I'd had. I needed to not think for a while, and bartending allows me to do that. Tomorrow, on the other hand, I needed to get ready to dive deep in and push through all the emotions.

CHAPTER 9

I HATE THOSE MORNINGS when you feel like you're waking up with a huge hangover but you didn't even drink the night before. The last few days had been like the first few days without Lucy. I felt like I couldn't go on, but I knew I must push on for her. She was always supportive in my quest to do right by people, and it's time that I did right by her.

I changed into my running clothes and headed out into the early morning breeze. It was still a bit chilly, but I liked it. My place is close to Central Park, so that was where I usually ran. The streets are always busy, but going into the park transports me away from the city, even if only for a little while. I loved living here because I like the constant movement of *everything*, but I like having my solitude from time to time as well. So, if I get my runs and meditation in, I feel much better.

Lucy used to do the early morning runs with me. It was our time to talk about work, friends, and anything else. We would keep a solid pace, enough to keep our hearts up, but not too fast that we couldn't talk. I missed that. I run faster now, head down, constant pace. I think it's because if I slow down, her ghost may catch up to me.

My thoughts were interrupted by my phone. It was a text from Lewis asking if I was ready to meet up yet. Of course, I wasn't, but I answered yes anyways and told them to come to my place in an hour. I shot Joe the same text as well.

I jogged back to my place. I got a pot of coffee brewing so it would be ready when they came, and I jumped in the shower. It was a good day for a cold shower, and as soon as the ice-cold water hit me, I was awake. When I needed to be focused and alert, a cold shower achieved that quickly. I soon was out of the shower.

As soon as I finished getting dressed, I heard a knock on the door, and then Lewis, Vanesa, and Joe all walked in. Lewis had doughnuts. Not my usual breakfast choice, but it's easy to eat while talking. I set out the coffee pot and three mugs for myself, Vanesa, and Joe. Lewis does not need any stimulants.

Joe started the conversation by saying, "I've already told Lewis and Vanesa about what we discussed yesterday."

"OK, thanks, Joe." I turned to Vanesa. "So, what did you find out at the law firm?"

"I've talked to the partners. They're willing to hire you as the investigators for the class action lawsuit. I brought the paperwork, and once you and Lewis sign it, I can discuss all the particulars. But Joe is not an investigator. I cannot discuss it with him," Vanesa stated.

I looked at Joe and said, "Hey, Joe, you want a part-time job? I always wanted a secretary."

Joe grinned and said, "Sure, bro, I'll be your secretary part-time."

"OK, great, now Joe is part of the investigation team. Vanesa, does that work for you?"

Vanesa laughed a little and said, "I'll write it into the paperwork. I just need you all to sign this, then we can get into specifics."

We all signed the document, which only covered anything pertaining to the company being sued, and waited for Vanesa to start.

"OK, guys, great. Now I can tell you more about the case. The company we are hitting with a class action lawsuit is Fibayson. They are the pharmaceutical giant behind the drug called Articus. It was supposed to be a groundbreaking drug to help people who are suffering from dementia, but it would also help prevent dementia. The drug could be prescribed to anyone eighteen and older. But Lucy discovered that this drug could cause tissue damage. While younger people may not be affected as much, for anyone with a tissue disorder or who was fifty and older, it could be fatal. Aging causes tissue to start breaking down, and most people with dementia are older. Therefore, this drug may help with dementia, but it starts causing tissue damage and people started dying. The drug manufacturer decided that rolling back all the pills they had already brought to market and were ready for sale would cost billions of dollars. In the end, they decided that it would be more beneficial to them if they continued moving forward, even though they knew the ramifications.

"The case was based off Lucy's reports, and she was the witness speaking for the victims. When she was killed, we knew there was still a case, but we needed more than just the research. We needed someone who could confirm the research. About a year after Lucy's murder, one of her co-researchers, Camila Jefferson, finally came to us. She knew what Lucy had been doing and wanted to help. We had tried convincing her earlier when we first started the case, but she was afraid of what would happen to her. But as the deaths from the drug continued to pile up, she could not consciously keep working for the company and wanted to help the victims. She had helped with developing Articus and knew about the research and agreed with Lucy's findings. That is why were able to reopen the case over the last few months. And it was then when I realized I was being followed and took off."

"OK, Vanesa, thanks for catching us up. My first question is, how are they continuing to produce this drug if people are dying?"

"Well, Angelo, it's simple really, and unfortunate. These people are older and already in stages of dementia, and no one has connected the extra tissue damage to their deaths. It's seen as a part of life, that we all will eventually die. Those with tissue disorders that took the drug, it just looks like their disorder came faster than anticipated, and they died from it. That's where the researcher comes in and proves that it is actually Articus causing these problems."

"Do you have protection for Camila?" Lewis asked.

"We have her in a relatively safe location, a house that one of the partners owns in his rental portfolio. There is an elevated police presence, but no round-the-clock protection."

Lewis stopped her there. "Just give me the details and I'll take care of the rest."

While Lewis and Vanesa went over the details for Camila, Joe looked at me and whispered, "Is this all for real? Lucy was targeted for murder?"

"I've only known for a couple of months, and you're hearing most of the details at the same time I'm learning them. I can't believe for over the last two years I just thought it was random, some horrible random crime. But it was a planned murder over something I had no idea about."

"I'm sorry, bro. This must be a lot right now. I'm here for you, and obviously, Lewis is too. Just tell me what to do."

"When we're done here, I'd like to talk to Nathan Grimble. Do you think you can make it happen?"

"Let me make some calls."

Joe stepped into the kitchen and got on his phone. Lewis and Vanesa were still talking. And there I was, left alone with my thoughts. My mind headed back to that night…before the murder.

CHAPTER 10

WE HAD JUST ENJOYED a nice dinner together. Chinese take-out that Lucy had picked up on her way home from work. She made sure that she was home early enough to have dinner with me before I had to go to work. She was always making sure that we had quality time together when we could. With my PI job and bartending on the side, sometimes we were on opposite schedules. But she could always figure out a way to get lunch, have an early dinner, or even a late-night snack at two in the morning if it meant we could talk.

We talked about her job and that she had some things coming up that may require some extra time. I was finishing up a big case that I had hoped to wrap up in the next week or two. We decided to plan a trip for when we were both done to St. Thomas for a week. We could get away for a while and disconnect from everything.

While I was gathering my things to head out, she grabbed me around the waist and gave me a huge hug. I turned around and gave her a kiss good night. As I was walking out, she said, "Stay safe out there," and she blew me a kiss. I wish I had told her the same.

▪ ▪ ▪

Lewis, Vanesa, and Joe were all standing around me in a circle, and I could tell they must have been trying to get my attention for a few seconds. Lewis said, "Are you back, Boss?"

"Yeah, yeah. Sorry. I was just…thinking."

Vanesa gave me a sympathetic look and said, "Let's be done for today. Lewis and I need to go set some things in motion."

"That's fine, I think Joe and I are going to meet with Nathan Grimble."

"Is that the fire investigator?" Lewis asked.

"He was the original fire investigator on the case before both cases were taken over by the NYPD," Joe answered, his anger simmering just below the surface.

As soon as Vanesa and Lewis left, Joe said, "Hey, just a heads-up, but my captain said he would like to sit in on this meeting. It's the only way he would let us talk to Grimble."

"No big deal, Joe. Probably better to have some oversight and another person hearing what he has to say. Where are we meeting?"

"At the firehouse, in the captain's office. We need to head out now. I was about to try and get us out of here before your little fade-out. What was that all about anyways?"

"I was just thinking about the night Lucy was murdered. We were just talking and having dinner. You know what she told me when I was leaving?" I paused, again lost in the memory. "Stay safe. The irony isn't lost on me."

"Sorry, bro. I'm sure all of this isn't easy on you. Let's go see if we can figure any of it out."

CHAPTER 11

AS JOE AND I strolled through the firehouse on our way to the captain's office, he was stopped a few times by other firefighters saying hello. He introduced me every time as his brother, the PI. We finally made it to the captain's office, and Nathan Grimble was already sitting there. He looked like he didn't want to be there. We all made introductions, and the captain started the meeting off by saying, "Nathan, we know you couldn't finish the investigation into both research lab fires, but we just want to get your take on your initial findings. This is nothing official and completely off the record."

That seemed to put Grimble at ease, at least more so than when we'd walked in. He picked up his messenger bag and pulled out two folders. After leafing through the papers, he pulled out one sheet from each folder and looked them over carefully. Nathan Grimble was a very serious old-timer. He had been the fire investigator for seven years, after being a firefighter for twenty-five. He still looked like he could put out a fire or two. When he finally spoke, it was very measured and with full intent. "OK, let's start with going over both fires together. Both fires had a very specific accelerant, ethyl alcohol. The police report stated that ethyl alcohol is standard in the research facilities and is used for different tasks, and that was why it was there. But from my interviews with the firefighters first on scene and even my initial walk-through when the fires were out, there was a significant amount of ethyl alcohol spread throughout the area."

Captain Brian Lamke asserted himself into the conversation, "Yes, my team was first on scene at both fires, and the smell was intense. We were lucky to make it back out before the entire building was engulfed. It was not just a few bottles from the lab—it was everywhere. Sorry for interrupting, Nathan; I just wanted to make sure that the point was made."

"Not a problem, Captain. Both research facilities are owned by the same company, Fibayson. And both fires' point of origin was in the records area. The only real difference in the fires was that there was an explosion in one of the buildings' laboratories. This was because this lab had just received a large shipment of methanol.

"In my initial findings, I had suspected arson, especially when the second fire occurred with almost the exact replication of the first. But, as you all already know, I was taken off the cases. Then the police fire investigator deemed both to be accidental from old wiring, case closed."

"Did you notice any old wiring during your investigation?" I asked.

Grimble shook his head and said, "Of course not. These buildings were all remodeled for the laboratories. They wouldn't have had old wiring being used."

All three of the men around me had gotten very tense. They'd all been on the job for far too long to be questioned in their beliefs concerning fires. I broke the brief silence with, "Thank you, Mr. Grimble, for meeting with us. And thank you,

Captain Lamke, for allowing me to hear this information. I'm not sure what Joe has told you, but my wife Lucy used to work in the second facility that was burned. She was murdered two years ago, and I'm not sure if there is a connection with this yet, but I promise to let you all in on what I find out. Again, thank you, and thank you for all you do for our city."

As we were leaving, Nathan Grimble caught up to us. He handed me his business card and said, "Mr. Barsotti, I'm sorry for your loss. If you need any help from me at all in your case, do not hesitate to call. I'm still upset and was blindsided when the police took over the case. I know my findings were on the track of arson, and I cannot begin to understand how they both were deemed accidental. I saw no wiring in either building near the origin spot. But I was also pulled before I could really dig into it."

He shook both of our hands and walked to his car. Joe turned to me and said, "We are all still upset by these cases. So, what do you think, bro?"

"I think that the fires are connected, but I'm not sure what the motive would be in the police covering up the arson. The fires started in the records department, so whoever started them must be trying to destroy evidence of any wrongdoing on the pharmaceutical company's part. The only other connection in both Lucy's murder and the fires is that the NYPD is where they aren't supposed to be. They had no reason to take over her murder or to take over the fire investigations.

"Let's head back to Lewis's. Hopefully he and Vanesa are back, and we can finish up today's earlier conversation."

"Sure, bro, just stay checked in this time!" Joe said as he laughed at his own joke way too hard.

CHAPTER 12

JOE AND I EXITED the cab at Lewis's building. It had been a weird ride over. The music was blaring so loud we couldn't even talk if we'd wanted to. The only time the cabbie turned it down was to get the address and to get payment. I'm surprised he could hear anything at all.

The door guy said hello to both of us as he opened the door. The receptionist, a friendly man named Javier, said that Miss Galloway and Mr. Pollard were five minutes out but that we could go up. I said, "Hey, Javier, you probably know more about me than even my brother here does. I've always wanted to know…how do you get all your information?"

"Well, Mr. Barsotti, when Mr. Pollard bought this building four years ago, he provided all of us with information packets. These packets have all our residents' pertinent information, so they feel more like friends every time they walk through these doors. He wants us to be able to communicate with the people living here and their frequent guests. It's rather extensive, but he tells us that he wants this to feel like a home they are coming to. Don't worry…all the information is available for public knowledge, no illegal information. Since he has taken over the building, we have had less than a five percent turnover rate because no one wants to leave, residents and employees alike. It has been amazing; he is an amazing person."

"That he is, Javier. Nice talking with you. We'll head up now."

Joe and I got on the elevator up to the penthouse, and Joe asked, "Lewis *owns* this building?"

"Apparently so. I didn't know."

I didn't know Lewis had bought this building, but it didn't surprise me how he treated his employees and residents. Lewis and I talk about a lot of things, but sometimes he keeps some of his business dealings to himself. I think it's more that he doesn't want to boast about the amount of money he has than not wanting me to know. What really makes Lewis amazing, though, is how he spreads his money to help take care of people and make things better. He is the least egocentric millionaire I have ever met.

We were met by Lewis's butler, and he handed us two ice-cold beers. He said that Lewis and Vanesa would be arriving shortly, and dinner would be ready in about an hour. After the first cold, crisp sip of the beer, the elevator dinged. Out walked Lewis, Vanesa, and another woman. She had beautiful brown skin and deep brown eyes, but she appeared scared.

Vanesa said, "Angelo, Joe, this is Camila Jefferson. Camila, this is Angelo Barsotti and his brother Joe."

Camila spoke softly, "Angelo, it's nice to finally meet you. I saw you at the funeral, but you were obviously upset, and I didn't want to intrude. I loved working with Lucy, and I miss her dearly."

"Thank you for saying that," I said. "I really appreciate you coming forward. I want to see justice for Lucy. I know after her death you must be very frightened. But now that you're here, I hope you feel safer. I know that Lewis is the right person to help protect you and your family through all of this. And we will do all we can to get the full story out there."

"I want justice for Lucy too, especially now I know that she was killed because of this." Camila seemed to gain her strength and confidence as she continued, "I also want justice for all the unnecessary deaths and people who have been hospitalized even though Lucy and I told them about the effects of Articus. We were just doing our jobs, and we did what we were supposed to do. Why would they do this?"

Vanesa interjected here and said, "Unfortunately, it always comes down to money. The company decided it was worth the potential lawsuits and risks versus pulling it off the market. They value human life significantly lower than most. It's a sad reality of big business."

Camila retorted back, "No, that's Big Pharma. They act like they want to save lives, but in reality, the sicker we get, the more money they make. The research department only exists so that the drugs don't kill everyone, and for appearances. I got into this job so that I could help people, but every time they don't listen to us, I wonder if I'm the problem."

"Of course, you're not the problem!" Lewis quickly jumped in. "People with money who are only striving to make more are the problem. And I should know. I have money, but I've made it my mission to help with my resources. Just as you joined the research facility to help make a difference. We can't always control what others do, but if we stay on track with our missions, we will never be the problem. We may sometimes cause problems for those who cannot see past the money, just like you're doing now. You coming forward will be a problem for Fibayson, but it is *their* problem they created, not yours."

"Thank you for saying that, Lewis. That's a great way to look at it. I've never met someone with your money to be so down-to-earth. You're a good one," Camila said, some calmness had returned to her voice.

Lewis looked a little embarrassed. He doesn't handle compliments very well. Blushing, he said, "Thank you, Camila. How about we all sit down to a nice meal that my chef has prepared for us? We can then discuss where we go from here."

CHAPTER 13

DINNER WAS LOVELY. IT was a nice break I think we all needed. And Lewis had conveniently seated me next to Vanesa. The chef had prepared crispy skin salmon with a teriyaki glaze, shaved brussels sprout salad, and fingerling potatoes with truffles and parmesan cheese. We all shared just one bottle of wine, a nice red from Lewis's collection, so that we were able to discuss the case further. Tonight was a night to focus, not let loose.

As the plates were being cleared, Joe started telling them about our meeting with Nathan Grimble. He filled them in on our thoughts and the coincidences. Lewis spoke up first, "Angelo, do you remember the NYPD being there at the investigation?"

"I do remember, Lewis, but I didn't really think anything of it at the time. Until now, I just thought it was normal. I'm rethinking a lot of that night now."

Vanesa said, "It seems that the NYPD is involved in all of this, but how are we supposed to get someone to talk?"

"I can talk to some people, but cops snitching on other cops it not going to be easy," Lewis said, shaking his head the whole time. "It will take some time and may not even prove to be useful in the end."

"Lewis, thanks. I know it won't be easy, but you have a way with people." Then to everyone else, he said, "I'll go through some of my old files and see who was on the scene and who questioned me right after. I think we need to start at the beginning and work from there. Joe, can you figure out how to get the file reports from the police? I would like to go over them before we question the police fire investigator."

Camila interrupted me and said, "What can I do to help?"

I told her, "You keep your family safe and tell your story in court. You're already risking a lot for this. You will be in constant contact with Vanesa and Lewis, and they can give you updates as we go along."

She seemed resigned about not having more involvement but didn't press the issue. I continued, "Vanesa, continue to work the class action. We need to bring all players involved out in the forefront. Lewis and I will start working the police angle as delicately as possible. And I know I don't have to say it, but I'm going to anyways: stay safe. If the police are tied up in this, things could get dangerous."

Lewis told everyone that they were welcome to stay at his place for the night, but only Vanesa and Camila did. Camila would go back with her family in the safe house Lewis arranged for them the next day. Joe wanted to go home to spend time with his son, and I needed my own bed and some time alone. The day was long, but it was only the beginning of the case. We had a lot to do, and many unfavorable situations lurked in our future. But this was for Lucy.

CHAPTER 14

THE SUN WAS SHINING, but my mood did not match it. Lewis had texted last night that he'd found a detective who would talk to us off the record. We were supposed to get lunch at the Shake Shack at noon. I hardly ever eat there anymore because the lines are huge, but we needed answers, and this was our first lead.

I thought back to the first time I took Lucy to the Shake Shack, before it was the chain that it grew into. It was originally a hot dog stand that operated just outside of Madison Square Park. The lines were manageable back then, but the word quickly spread how good the food was. In 2004, it changed its name to what has now become an icon and spreading chains throughout the U.S.

Lucy and I had just finished our run in the midafternoon. We liked to sleep in on the weekend and get up and go for a run then share lunch together, when my schedule allowed it. I told her we were going to a new hot spot for lunch. As we neared the hot dog stand, she gave me a disappointed look. I told her, "Just wait."

As soon as she took her first bite, she told me she was sorry she ever doubted me. We had made it a routine to go there once a month—the food was that good—and it gave us extra walking time. It became one of our "spots."

I decided to follow that same routine today. I would do our normal run through Central Park and then walk the 1.8 miles to Madison Square Park. I ran harder that day than usual; I was running for both of us. As I exited Central Park, Lewis was waiting for me. I wasn't surprised. I had told Lewis that I was going for a run, and I would meet him at Madison Square Park. But Lewis must have remembered about Lucy and my routine and decided I could use someone to walk with.

"Hey, Boss, I figured I would find you here. You care if I join you on your walk over?"

"Sure, Lewis. I can't believe you remember about my routine with Lucy. Well, actually, I do believe it, so what I'm trying to say is, thanks for being a good friend."

He acknowledged my gratitude with an arm around my shoulders. I asked him, "So, who are we meeting? And why here?"

"First off," Lewis said, "no last names. Obviously, I know who he is, but he wants to keep it to first names with anyone else. And he wants to meet here because we will just be people standing in line to get lunch and just happen to be talking. We'll all get food and be on our separate ways. The long line should give us sufficient time to discuss."

The line was down the block. Lewis and I got in line and waited. And waited. We had been in line for twenty minutes and were about halfway through when Lewis received a text message. He looked up at me and said, "He's not coming."

CHAPTER 15

ON THE WALK BACK to my apartment, Lewis told me that his contact thought he was being followed. He still said that he would meet us, but not there. He would contact us when he could. We were almost back to my apartment when Lewis got a call. When he hung up, he said, "My driver picked up our guy. We'll take a ride around town and get some answers, hopefully. He'll meet us around the corner from your place in five minutes."

"How?" These were the only words I could muster.

"When I met up with you, I had my driver be on the lookout for our guy. When he spotted him, he followed him. When I got the text that he wasn't coming, my driver picked him up. Plan B, Boss. Always have one." He laughed a little as I shook my head in amazement.

We walked around to the back of my apartment building and found Lewis's driver waiting for us. There was a man in the back seat, but he was covered head to toe. He had sunglasses, a hat, a scarf wrapped around his face, and baggy clothing. He was concealing his identity, but he sure stuck out like a sore thumb. Lewis climbed into the back seat, and I took the passenger seat. The driver pulled out into the NYC traffic.

Lewis said, "Angelo, this is John."

John just nodded his head. I said, "Nice to meet you, John."

"What happened back there, John?" Lewis asked.

John began talking in a scruffy voice, but it was obvious it wasn't his natural tone. He said, "I thought I was being followed. And then when your driver stopped me, I thought I had been caught. Luckily, he explained very quickly what we were going to do, and I hopped in."

"Well, John, with how you're dressed, someone, everyone, probably thought you were a bomber or some other nefarious type. You look ridiculous!" Lewis laughed.

"Lewis, you know that talking about cops can get me in serious trouble, or worse."

I decided since he brought it up, I would follow it with a question, "So, John, what is it that you have?"

"Well, there are some bad things going on in the NYPD. It isn't all of us, or even most of us, but there are some who are taking money to 'look the other way,' if you know what I mean."

"As in bribes?" I clarified. "How do you know this for sure?"

"There is a group inside the homicide division, and when they catch a case, they all get involved in it. I think there are three or four in this group. They've all been there a long time and are always together.

"I know about it because one night I was working late when one of them got a call for a case. He looked at me and said, 'I'm a man short tonight. Can you help us out on this one?' I had heard the rumors, but I didn't know anything for sure, and I couldn't just say no to helping. So, I went with them. It was a murder case, but when we got there, there was some-one there that I had never seen before. He handed the detective who had asked me to come along a bag. The detective unzipped it and quickly closed it back up. The man left, but I had seen cash in the bag before it was closed.

"I decided right then and there that I did not want any part of whatever was going to happen next. I faked an emergency call from my wife and said that she had gone into labor. They told me I was good to go, and I got out of there.

"Thankfully, they let it go with that. They've never asked me to go out on a call with them again. I won't give up any names, but hopefully this helps you understand how some things happen around there."

I said, "You had said three or four. Why aren't you sure how many?"

"I passed up my opportunity to join them about a year ago. They must be looking to add another guy because they continued asking other detectives to take cases with them. There were three, but recently a newer detective to the force—he's an older guy but transferred to the NYPD about eight months ago—started regularly going out on cases with them.

"OK, guys, I've given you what I came to say, and I did this as a favor to Lewis. Please do not contact me again, and whatever you do, you didn't get any information from a cop. Please… lives could be at stake."

"But what about the lives and cases that are being compromised by these guys running around rogue?" I asked, raising my voice as he continued to get out of the car.

"Sorry," is all he said as he briskly walked away. We weren't even at a complete stop when he got out, and now he was gone.

CHAPTER 16

ON THE WAY BACK to my apartment, Lewis said, "I'll work on trying to figure out some names. At the very least, I'm sure I can get a list of homicide detectives, and we can work the names and narrow it down."

"Thanks, Lewis. I know you will. I just can't stop thinking about how this is all coming out now. If we had all this information right when Lucy was killed, we could've solved this a while ago. Now it's hitting me all over again."

"I know this is hard on you. Just know I am here for you, and so are your brother and Vanesa," Lewis said while putting his hand on my shoulder.

His driver pulled around to the front of my apartment, and I got out. I told Lewis thanks again, and I thanked his driver for everything he did as well. I told them that I would see them tomorrow.

When they pulled away, I decided to take a walk. I needed a new perspective. I wanted to let my thoughts guide me. I wasn't even sure where I was headed, but I walked with purpose and knew I was going to get to where I needed to be.

I had walked aimlessly for miles, without any sense of direction. When I looked up to see where I was, there was

Magnolia Bakery. I hadn't been here since Lucy had died. We would always come here when we needed a sweet treat. It was her favorite! Even before *Sex and the City* made it the talk of the town. It's right around the corner from McGinty's, but I always found a way to avoid it. Why was I here now?

I decided since I was here, I would go in and order my favorite cupcake, the red velvet cupcake. I got two, out of habit. Lucy and I would always get the same thing. I sat at a table alone with two giant cupcakes staring back at me. Then someone approached from behind me and asked, "Is someone joining you?"

I couldn't turn around fast enough. I knew that voice. It couldn't be! But it was. I couldn't even form words as he just gazed at me and said, "I've been looking for you."

CHAPTER 17

"WHAT ARE YOU DOING here? Why are you not in jail?" I asked, getting loud. People started looking at us.

"Angelo, we need to talk. I have some things to tell you. And now that everyone else is listening as well, maybe we could go somewhere else?"

"Why would I trust you? You're a traitor to the badge!" Now *everyone* was watching the scene.

"Look, Angelo, here is my badge. I still have it, so I need to fill you in on why." He leaned in and whispered, "I also think we are working the same case again, and I can be of some help."

I glanced around. People were waiting for my reaction. Begrudgingly, I grabbed a to-go box, packed up my things, and walked outside. When he followed me out, I turned to look him straight in the eyes and said, "I don't know what strings you pulled, Detective Tanner, but I still don't trust you!"

He put his hands up and said, "I get that, but hear me out, and I think you will eventually get back to believing in me again."

I muttered, "I doubt it. But go on…convince me."

"Let me start by apologizing," Detective Tanner said. "I didn't want to deceive you and Lewis, but I had to keep my cover. I'm not actually a police detective for the NYPD. I work for Internal Affairs. I am still undercover because of the things going on in the NYPD. What you saw with Grant Dogon was me trying to get in with a group of detectives that we have identified as being dirty. The problem is, we haven't been able to figure out yet who is contributing to their funds. Someone or a group is behind the money that they're getting to cover up certain crimes, and that's why I was brought in. I know this is a lot to take in, so do you have any questions before I continue?"

I had stopped walking midway through his declaration and was in complete astonishment. I asked, "But I read in the newspapers that you went to trial and were convicted. How can you explain that?"

"Well, because I pulled that stunt with Grant, the other detectives decided I was on their side and with them. Some higher-ups got all the charges dropped and reinstated me without incident. Obviously, I had to pull some of the strings as well, but in the end, it was like nothing happened. The next day I walked back into the department. Are you with me so far?"

I couldn't think of any other rational possibilities of how he could be out of jail and still have a badge, so he must be telling me the truth. I said to him, "I'm with you, but my trust in you still needs reconstructing. You will have to earn that."

"I get it, Angelo, and I hope to do just that. It's why I sought you out tonight. I wanted to explain myself and hopefully help you with solving Lucy's murder."

"What could you know about that?" I started getting angry again. "That was over two years ago, and you said you just began working with these guys within the last year, and really just the last few months. Explain."

"Your timeline is correct, but there have been some fires recently that came to our dirty detectives. I was only with them for one, but I overheard some things. And I have been doing some digging into their old cases to help make our case against them. Your wife's murder was one of the old cases."

The connection between the fires and Lucy's murder was put at the forefront once again. My head was spinning; again, there were too many connections to be a coincidence. I needed and wanted to talk to Detective Tanner more, but I needed Lewis and Joe here too. I didn't think I could handle this one on my own. I was too close to the situation. I said, "Tanner, I believe you. In this messed up world, your story makes sense. But if we're going to go down this road, I need my team with me. And before we can go talk to them, I need to tell Lewis everything you just told me. Otherwise, if you just walked in, he may punch you right in the mouth. Can I have a day to get everyone on the same page, and we can meet in a more formal setting?"

"Sure, Angelo, take the day. But things are heating up with this, and I want to make sure we have all the answers before these guys go down. They may not be as talkative when they get locked up."

"Understood."

CHAPTER 18

I CALLED EVERYONE TOGETHER to gather at Lewis's for a meeting. I didn't tell them why, just that I had a break in the case that we needed to discuss. We had assembled in an hour, with everyone waiting for me to speak.

I started by saying, "I was approached today by a detective in the NYPD, and he has information on the group of dirty detectives Lewis and I heard about earlier. To fill some of you in first, Lewis and I met with one of his contacts who told us that there was a group of detectives being paid by some unknown organization to cover up certain crimes. He knows firsthand that they have done this on at least one case that he was present for.

"Then after we had met this man, I was approached. Some of us know this detective, and there are going to be some questions, but I want you all to know that I believe him." I addressed Joe, "We'll fill you in later on our backstory with this detective, but for now, just trust me."

Lewis stood up and said, "Love the suspenseful buildup, Boss, but can you just tell us who you're talking about here?"

"I'm getting there, Lewis, I promise. But I want to fill you in on what he's bringing to the table first. He has worked with this group of detectives and has seen what they have done. He also worked with them on one of the research facility fires. He knows the cops involved and wants to work with us."

"Why would he be willing to give up his own so easily?" Vanesa asked. "And how does he even know we're pursuing this angle?"

"Well, he's Internal Affairs, working undercover. As for how he knows, I'm not sure. If we decide to work with him, we can ask. But I came to all of you first because we all must be in agreement. And once I say his name, you will have the same reservations I did at first."

I waited for a bit, just to make Lewis anxious. He hates having to wait, and I like messing with him when I can. Finally, I said, "It's Detective Tanner."

The wind was taken out of the room. Lewis and Vanesa sat there, mouths open wide and disbelief in their eyes. Joe had no idea what was happening.

Eventually, Vanesa and Lewis's shock turned to anger. Both asked multiple questions all at once. "How can we trust him…?" "He betrayed us…" "Why is he not in jail…?" "I'd like to show him how I really feel about him…"

I put both hands up and said, "Listen, I obviously wouldn't have even brought this to you all if I didn't believe what he had to say. I think you both need to hear it from him to get a full sense of this. But also, he said that he has been researching these detectives' old cases to build his own case, and one of them is Lucy's murder. So, feelings aside, will you at least hear what he has to say?"

After much hesitation, they both agreed. I texted Tanner that we could meet tomorrow morning. He responded that would work, as he was on nights. I also wanted to give Lewis and Vanesa a night to sleep on their emotions. It would give me time to fill Joe in on the Tanner story.

CHAPTER 19

WE ALL DECIDED IT was easiest to all stay at Lewis's and discuss the situation in the morning before Tanner came by. Once Lewis and Vanesa went to bed, Joe came up to me and asked, "What was that all about?"

I went through the whole ordeal from the Craig Mazer case and everything that followed. I also explained to him how Tanner approached me and why I would choose to trust him now. He agreed with me and felt it was our best lead.

When Joe went to bed, I was alone with my thoughts again. I wished Joe and I saw more of each other. We think along the same lines, and we get each other. We have always been there when the other needed help, but we should have a better relationship outside of that. Lucy always made sure that we got together regularly, but since her passing it has been rare. She was the glue in my life, and I was still trying to collect all the pieces that came apart.

■ ■ ■

I had fallen asleep on the couch. Lewis's butler woke me when he arrived at 5 a.m. All his staff live in the building rent free. I walked back to the bedroom and decided to take a quick nap in bed to get rid of the body aches I had gained while sleeping upright.

I tried for thirty minutes to sleep, but it didn't happen for me. I was worried about how the meeting with Tanner would go. I really needed everyone to be onboard. And I wanted to get moving on this now.

I wanted to go for a run but had no clothes to change into, and I didn't want to wake Lewis up to ask. I settled for a cup of coffee on the balcony. It was cold enough outside to wake me up and get me going.

I started going over in my head how I thought this would play out with Tanner seeing Lewis and Vanesa. He never even met Vanesa, but she sure knows about him, or what she thought she knew. I needed to make sure that everyone heard Tanner out before they came to conclusions.

Suddenly, I was back sitting on my porch the night of Lucy's murder. I saw detectives all around asking me questions, and everything was blurry. The words were all jumbled and didn't make any sense. The only thing I could see was the emblem of the NYPD on the officers' jackets.

Having dozed off, I jolted upright and realized I must have been more tired than I'd thought. I was still on the balcony, but someone had put a blanket on me. I looked at my watch; it was 7:30. I was out for almost two hours, and I was cold. When I came inside, everyone was sitting around the table. Lewis said, "Glad you could join us, Boss. Detective Traitor should be here soon."

"Lewis, please, before you start with hostility, listen with an open mind. I think once you hear all he has to say, you'll understand everything."

"We'll see about that," Lewis muttered.

CHAPTER 20

WE HAD ALL FINISHED eating breakfast when Detective Tanner texted that he was downstairs. Lewis called down and told them to send him up. Everyone was on pins and needles as we heard the whir of the elevator coming up. It pinged and out stepped Detective Tanner holding a box.

Tanner looked around with an awestruck look on his face. He said, "Wow, Lewis, I'm impressed."

"Forget the pleasantries, Detective, let's hear what you have to say," Lewis said with a mild temperament, but we all got the point.

Detective Tanner said, "I understand you still being upset Lewis. If someone had done to me what I did to you all, I'd be upset too. But I promise there was a reason, and it's not what you may think."

Tanner went through the whole story as he had with me. They asked the same questions I did. I could see their faces change as he went through it, and after he had answered each question thoroughly, I sensed the room change.

Lewis stood up and walked over to Detective Tanner. Everyone was watching and waiting for what Lewis would do.

He stood right in front of Tanner and finally put out his hand, saying, "I believe you."

"Thanks for understanding. I really just want to put these guys away, but we need to figure out who is funding the operation," Detective Tanner said.

"Hey, Tanner, what's in the box?" I asked.

"Right. Well, I was hoping this would go like it did, and I brought the old case files of these detectives that I've been investigating. Every case that they have worked on is in there, along with a copy of my notes. Most of the cases are normal, run-of-the-mill stuff, with no irregularities that I noticed. In a separate file, there are the other cases they've worked on, and they go against everything a normal case would conclude. For example, with your wife's murder, they had no reason to be on the case. It should have been local authorities handling the case, but they took it over. They were also on the scene too quickly, like they knew the call was coming. Usually, if the locals want help from a larger police force, the call goes out and they are on it the following day. But they were there questioning you, Angelo, the same night.

"There are many cases in there just like it, but I wanted you all to look through and see what you come up with and get your impressions. I've looked through with a police procedural mind, so I want your take. Obviously, I hope this goes without saying, but this is very sensitive material and cannot leave this apartment without me being the one to take it out. I'll leave it here for a few days, and on my next day off, we can compare notes. Does that work for all of you?"

Everyone nodded their heads, and Detective Tanner turned and left. Everyone's faces were a mix of shock and excitement.

They all knew what Tanner had put us through before, but this could be a major turning point in our search for justice.

CHAPTER 21

WE OPENED THE BOX and pulled out the smaller folder of the two. The cases were each separated by a small binder clip, and we each took one and began to look through each case separately. Vanesa had taken an armored truck robbery case. Lewis took an arson case at one of the research facilities, and Joe took the other arson case. I took the file marked "Lucy Barsotti."

I went through the case thoroughly, as if I hadn't seen it before. I knew what everything should say, so I thought it best that I took this one. But reading each word sparked the pain inside me. I was crying before I finished the first page. I pushed past the pain. I needed to see what was off about this case, and why Tanner had marked this one as suspicious besides what he had said.

The first few pages were straightforward with what a police report should look like. They had marked home invasion and a murder. One victim, female. No suspects at time of final report. I got to the notes section. These were the police's initial findings on the scene. As I read through the notes, I noticed some faint writing in the margin. It was a copy, and the writing looked like it had been erased, but I could make out what it said:

Professional Hit

That wasn't in the report anywhere. Why would someone write that and not follow up that lead? And what made them think that?

I pushed that to the side and focused on the rest of the notes. Obviously, my name was throughout both detectives' notes, but I was cleared quickly with the number of traffic cams in New York City where I was doing my investigation.

While I waited for everyone else to finish reading their cases, I went back through the report again. I wrote down the detectives' names and tried searching anywhere in the report where it may hint at a professional hit. I couldn't find it anywhere.

Vanesa was the first to speak up, and as I looked up to listen, I noticed everyone was done reviewing their case. "Well, the armored truck robbery was solved by the detectives, but the count was over $100,000 short of what was supposed to be in the truck. It was deemed a loss, and the detectives were not suspected of foul play."

Lewis said, "These guys were on the arson case right away. In the report, it states that they arrived before firefighters. There is no reason given as to why they took over the case from the fire investigator, just that the police fire investigator deemed it accidental to faulty wiring."

"That's not right! We were first on scene in both fires. I can't be one hundred percent sure on the arson case you have, Lewis, but it says the same exact thing in mine. But I was there, and we were definitely first on the scene," Joe said, getting more upset with each word.

"Joe, did you notice anything else in the case file?" I asked. "I know it's hard to look at when it all doesn't make sense, trust me, but we need to dig in and get everything sorted."

"I understand, bro. It's just so frustrating. The only other thing I noticed was that ALL files were destroyed in the fire. It doesn't track with what I saw. We had gotten the fire under control rather quickly, especially with the amount of accelerant. But I cannot say for sure because the case was taken away from us."

Lewis said, "This one said the same—all records destroyed. How about you, Boss? I'm sure that wasn't an easy read."

"It was hard, but I want justice. I noted what Tanner had said but focused on the rest. And I couldn't find anything else out of the ordinary."

I'm not sure why I held back the detective's note I found, but I did. I wouldn't keep it from Lewis for long, but I didn't want to discuss that with the group right now. I wanted to move through the other files Tanner brought and start getting to work.

We continued the same process for each one of the cases that Detective Tanner had separated out. We moved on to the other folder, just to make sure Detective Tanner hadn't missed anything.

CHAPTER 22

WE SPENT THE REST of the day going through every file and discussing each thing we found. We then went through the same files again but each taking different cases than we'd read before to gain a different perspective.

After working through lunch, we all realized we were starving and a break was necessary. Lewis took us all out to Mastero's for dinner. When we finished eating and drinking a bottle of wine, Lewis said, "We need to look into these detectives. There are four names that continue to show up in each of the files and we will confirm with Detective Tanner that the names are correct and that we are looking into the right people. This won't be an easy task, as police are the hardest to investigate, so we will need to be very careful."

"You're right, Lewis, so I suggest that you and I take on that task alone," I stated. "If anyone will have the police on their bad side, it will be us. Vanesa and Joe, with your professions, you need to stay clear of the police side of all this. Vanesa, I think you should continue with the case against Fibayson. And Joe, if you want to further your investigation into the arson cases, then we'll help you with that. Lewis and I will keep you up-to-date on what we find."

"I'm OK with that, but you must be careful," Vanesa said, looking like she wanted to say more, but held back.

Joe put up a bit of a fight, but in the end, he knew that he had to work with the police day in and day out with his job. Lewis said he would get his team on the backgrounds of these guys as soon as I got the green light from Tanner.

I took out my phone and sent Tanner a text message:
Domingo, Chance, Waverly, and Grims. Confirm?

Joe and I decided to go to our own homes that night and get a good night's sleep. We decided to split a cab to get us there. Lewis offered a driver to come get us, but we declined.

I turned to Vanesa, "Hey, last time we left here, you disappeared. Let's not do that again, OK?" Everyone got a little laugh out of that as Joe and I got into the cab.

As we pulled away, Joe turned to me and said, "I know why I needed to go home tonight, as I start my 48-hour shift tomorrow. But it seems like you and Vanesa have some kind of connection. I've noticed multiple times how you have looked at each other? Am I missing something?"

"We do have a connection, but my mind needs one hundred percent focus on the task at hand. I cannot let distractions interfere with justice for Lucy. If the connection is still there when this is over, I will definitely pursue it."

"OK, bro. She likes you for sure, so I just wanted to make sure you weren't too daft to notice."

CHAPTER 23

I was woken up by my phone ringing. It was 2:30 a.m. Even though the screen was a little fuzzy to my bleary eyes, I could see it was Detective Tanner. I answered, "Hello?"

"Angelo, sorry to wake you. I thought I'd get voice mail."

"It's fine. What did you need?"

"We're on another case, and it has already gone sideways. I came with Domingo on this one because no one else was in. He told me on the way over that I wasn't to say a word, just watch his six. When we got to the scene, a man had been murdered. He was strangled, but it looked like he had been waterboarded before that. There was a metal table set up with a barrel of water and rags that were soaking wet. The killer was still there…" He hesitated. "He was waiting on Domingo to get there. He handed Domingo a bag of cash and told him to clean it up and make sure no one found the body. Domingo handed me the cash and told me to grab his red bag out of the trunk, and I called as soon as I stepped out of the building."

I asked him, "Did you recognize either the killer or the guy that was killed?"

"I've never seen the killer before, he just looks like somebody's muscle, but…" his voice trailed off.

It took him a few seconds to talk again. "The guy they murdered was Nathan Grimble, the NYPD fire investigator."

I was in disbelief. Maybe I heard him wrong, or I just wasn't awake enough. I said, "Can you repeat the last part? Did you say Nathan Grimble?"

"Yes, but I really need to get back inside before Domingo sees me on my phone or starts wondering where I am. I thought I'd just be leaving you a quick voice mail to call me. We'll talk soon, but I must go. Just be careful," he said hurriedly before he hung up.

Sleep was impossible at that point. Every time I tried to close my eyes, I saw Nathan Grimble being waterboarded. He was just doing his job; he should not have been killed. I shot Joe and Lewis each a text that said:

Call when you get up, I'll be awake.

CHAPTER 24

IT WAS FINALLY MORNING. Well, at least the sun was finally out. It had been morning since Tanner called. I sat around not doing anything, while trying to do everything I could to keep my mind from how Grimble was murdered.

Joe was the first to call. I told him about Tanner's phone call and what he said had happened. Joe was in a state of shock, I knew, because I had to call out his name multiple times to get him to say anything back to me. I explained to him that he needed to keep this information to himself; otherwise, Tanner would be exposed. Joe said he understood, but I wasn't so sure how he'd handle being in the firehouse over the next two days. I told him I'd be meeting with Tanner and would try to find out more. He said he needed to go.

While I was waiting for Lewis or Tanner to call, I decided to go for a run. I got ready and jogged out of my complex. But my body was tired from lack of sleep and mental exhaustion. I figured it was best to still get some exercise, but a walk would have to do.

I went to Lucy's favorite thinking spot, a hidden gem in New York, the Green-Wood Cemetery. It's a twenty-five-minute cab ride from my place, but I needed it. I always thought it was a creepy place to go alone and think, but when she finally allowed me to come with her, I figured out what was so special there. The history alone gives the place a special feel, but the tranquility of the place in the middle of Brooklyn is amazing.

Our first trip there together was when we were debating having children. She said we needed to get outside of our normal element and feel what's inside us. She had told me the history of the cemetery on the ride over, so that when we got there, I could just soak it in. She told me that when she came here, she would walk until she felt compelled to stop. Lucy said that something about this place would always give her clarity when she needed it. So, we split up and just walked. I could feel the stillness in the air, and everything was calm. I had been so anxious with the thought of having children, but as I explored, I was able to see a future where we had children and a full family. I never stopped to think, but that is probably more my need to move than anything else, but I did feel the power of the Green-Wood. It was that day that we decided to move out of the city and try and start a family.

I had been to the cemetery a few times since Lucy's passing, usually when trying to deal with the grief. This day was different; I needed guidance on whether I was pursuing this case for selfish reasons or if I was trying to help all involved. There was so much danger already in what we had found out so far, so more was sure to come. I walked and walked and let the stillness wash over me again. I knew what I needed to do.

Lewis had called while I was walking the cemetery, so I texted him that I would come over to his place. I told him we needed to talk, that Tanner had woken me up at 2:30 in the morning with disturbing news. Of course, he wanted to discuss right away, but when he tried calling, I just answered with, "I'll be there soon."

CHAPTER 25

THE MORNING RUSH WAS still in full swing when I took a cab to Lewis's. It gave me time to reflect on Lucy and the Green-Wood. I thought about how many decisions we had made there, and how many she must have made before she took me. I am forever grateful that she showed me because it still gives me a quiet retreat from the city.

When the cab pulled up to the building, I paid the driver and headed up to the penthouse. I stopped to say hello to the doorman and the attendant on duty. When the doors opened at the penthouse, I could smell coffee and breakfast. I realized at that moment that I was starving. I had been up since Tanner's call and hadn't eaten anything.

As Lewis's chef prepared me a plate of food, Lewis came in from the terrace and asked, "What's going on?"

"Let me grab my food and some coffee, and I'll join you and Vanesa on the terrace."

When I sat down with my plate, they stared and waited for me to shove some of the delicious food in my mouth. Finally, I said, "Tanner called at 2:30 a.m. and was in the middle of a job with Domingo. They were called out to a murder, but they weren't there to solve it but make it go away."

"Tanner is covering up murders now?" Vanesa asked, shocked.

I continued, "Unfortunately the man was already dead, and Tanner needs to keep his cover for now. But that's not the worst part. The dead guy was Nathan Grimble."

I let this piece of information hang in the air, leaving Vanesa and Lewis speechless. Neither of them had met the man but knew who he was and that Joe knew him well. Eventually, Lewis asked, "Is there anything we can do? What does this mean?"

"Well, I haven't talked to Detective Tanner since he called, but I think that Mr. Grimble continued working the fires and wanted to prove his arson theories. When we met with him, he wasn't too happy about being pulled off both cases and to have his theories completely dismissed. I don't know this for sure, but why else would he be killed and his murder covered up? It also means that we need to be even more careful about who we trust and who we talk to."

"Got it, Boss," Lewis said as Vanesa nodded her head.

"Lewis, I need you to get as much information on these detectives as soon as possible. We need to be careful, but we need to act quickly so no one else gets hurt."

"I'm on it. I'll get some extra help on this one too," Lewis said as he went inside to make some calls.

Vanesa turned to me and asked, "Are you working at the bar tonight?"

"No, I have some extra time off. Roy is being generous because he knows what this case means to me."

"Can we forget about all the death and troubles for the night then?" she asked. "Will you take me to dinner tonight?"

"I think that can be arranged. I need to go home and shower and take a quick nap, but I'm sure Lewis can set something up…again."

She laughed, stood up, and gave me a hug. As she was about to go inside, she said, "See you at seven."

CHAPTER 26

I APPRAISED MYSELF IN the mirror and decided I looked good enough. I had been through so much, but I thought that I had pulled myself together enough to pass as normal for the night. I had also decided that I'd focus on the future tonight.

Vanesa texted that she was outside. Lewis had given us a car, a driver, and reservations at Gramercy Tavern. I walked outside where Vanesa was standing next to the car. She took my breath away. She was wearing a lavender dress that fit her perfectly and brought out those blue eyes. After she gave me a hug, I opened the door for her.

We rode to the restaurant and talked about Detective Tanner and how crazy it was that he was involved with us again. Then we decided that would be the last we talked of the case, and it was.

We arrived at Gramercy Tavern and the atmosphere was amazing. White tablecloths draped over all the tables, and antique lighting provided a romantic glow. The cozy place offered a seasonal five-course tasting menu along with wine pairings. And Lewis had of course secured us a private table in the back. We did, however, get to order for ourselves this time.

We decided to get one of each item off the tasting menu, paired with the appropriate wines.

While we waited for our first course, I asked Vanesa, "Where did you grow up? I know where you went to college and law school, but tell me about the early years."

"Well, I grew up in Cincinnati, Ohio. My mother and father still live there."

"Any siblings?"

As she was about to answer, our first course came along with our wine pairing. I said, "Don't worry, we'll come back to that. Let's enjoy this while it's hot."

We had a light conversation about how good the food was, and that while a nice white wine was a good start, we were waiting for the reds. The second course came right as we finished the first.

When we finished the second course, I said, "So, siblings?"

She said, "I had two brothers and a sister, but only one brother and my sister are still with us." She began tearing up, but quickly recovered.

"I'm so sorry. Do you mind me asking what happened?"

She took a long time to answer. I think she was making sure that she didn't lose it while talking. She finally replied, "Actually, we lost him around the same time you lost Lucy. He was killed in a tragic car accident."

She let this linger, and I thought about how hard I had taken Lucy's death and still do. I also thought about Joe and how I would be if I lost him.

She continued, "His name was Julian. He was my older brother, and the oldest of the four."

The third course arrived quicker than I had expected. Lewis has that effect on restaurant service. Even though he wasn't there, he was the one to make the reservations. So, before we started eating, I reached over and held Vanesa's hand and said, "I'm really sorry for your loss. I know how hard it can be, as you know. I wish you would have shared this with me earlier. I could have helped you through the pain."

She thanked me and gave me a kiss on the check. She said, "I know you would have, but I didn't want to add to the pain you were already feeling."

I called the waiter over. "Can we please have a bottle of your Great Sage Cabernet?"

He said, "Of course, but the wine pairing for this dish is what is recommended by the chef."

"I understand, but we like red, and we would like to start drinking that now."

As he left to get the bottle, I said quietly to Vanesa, "I'm sure the chef won't like hearing about this, but what can I say? I'm a rebel. I like my fish with red."

She nodded in agreement as we shared a nice laugh. It was good to see her smile. Once we had our wine, we were more relaxed, and the conversation flowed throughout the rest of dinner. By the time dessert came, we decided it was best to have it boxed up, and we could share it later.

CHAPTER 27

WHEN WE ENTERED LEWIS'S building, the desk attendant said that Mr. Pollard was out for the evening, and we could expect him back tomorrow at some time. We thanked him and took the elevator to the penthouse.

It was quiet when we walked into the main room. Apparently, the staff was out for the evening as well. A note was propped against an ice bucket chilling a bottle of champagne on the coffee table. The note read:

I hope that you two enjoy having the place to yourselves. I have given the staff the night off and I have made other arrangements for the night. I will see you both tomorrow.

We shared a nervous giggle, and I grabbed the bucket with the champagne and two glasses and headed for the terrace. Vanesa followed with our desserts from the restaurant. We sat in the patio loveseat and enjoyed the champagne, our treats, and each other's company.

The conversation was light and somewhat flirtatious. Vanesa likes to talk with her hands quite often, and she touched my arm and rested her hand on my knee when I would talk. Eventually, I grabbed her hand in mine and pulled her head toward me so we could share our first kiss. I would swear Lewis was watching from somewhere because fireworks started going off in the distance right when it happened.

It was a nice way to end the night. We were both tired and had a fair amount to drink during the evening. We also knew what was at stake in the coming days. We were both grateful for the break and glad to resolve at least some of the tension between us. We walked inside hand in hand, and I gave her a kiss on the cheek before she headed to her bedroom.

I went to my room—well, the room reserved for me at Lewis's—and lay down. As my head hit the pillow, I was still lingering in that moment when those fireworks went off as we kissed. I was convinced Lewis was behind it, but either way, it was perfect.

I fell asleep fully clothed, still feeling Vanesa's lips on mine.

CHAPTER 28

I **AWOKE TO NOISES** in the main room. It was just the chef preparing breakfast. I could smell the eggs and bacon from my bed. I peered at my watch through blurry eyes; it was 8:30. I couldn't tell you the last time I slept that late, but it had been a big night. I was about to get dressed when I realized I was still in my clothes from the previous night. I would have headed out in my wrinkled clothes until I noticed a pile of clothes sitting in the lounge chair. They were a pair of shorts and a T-shirt, and they were mine. I didn't remember bringing them, but I put them on anyways. When I reached the bottom of the pile, there was another note from Lewis:

I packed you a change of clothes...hope you had fun.

I walked out to the living room to see who else was awake. I saw Vanesa seated at the table finishing up her breakfast. She smiled at me and asked me to join her. I sat down, and the chef must have heard me because he had a plate of food and a cup of coffee headed my way. When he set it down, I couldn't believe it. It was just bacon and eggs, but the immaculate presentation made it seem like a five-star breakfast.

Vanesa stood up and said, "Let's go for a walk."

I said, "I just started eating, and you just asked me to sit with you."

"I know, but I'll go change while you finish up. I need to talk to you about some things that I was thinking about last night."

I was confused but nodded and went back to eating the perfect eggs and bacon. I couldn't help but wonder what this talk would be about.

▪ ▪ ▪

We headed out of the building doors and started walking down the city block. The morning rush was almost over, but the streets were still packed with honking cars and loud sounds coming from everywhere. We walked about a block and a half before Vanesa finally said, "I was thinking about Lucy before I went to bed last night."

I stopped and said, "That's a little weird. Why were you thinking about her?"

"Sorry, I should have phrased that differently," she said, blushing embarrassment. "I was thinking about how they found out that she was my key witness. That was sealed and to be kept anonymous until the trial, as it could put her life in danger."

"Right, I understand, and I'm assuming you didn't tell anyone, correct?"

She said quickly, "No, of course not! That's why I don't understand how they found out."

"Who is this 'they' you are referring to?" I asked.

"OK, I'm not one hundred percent sure who, but 'they' did contact me. It was from a blocked number, and they spoke using a digitally altered voice. The voice said that if I didn't tell them who my witness was, that I would not like what would happen."

"What happened next? You said you didn't tell them, but they still found Lucy. Why are you just now telling me this?"

"Angelo, I immediately went to the partners at my firm, and we proceeded with filing a protective action for Lucy. But we were too late. The day we filed the protection detail with the judge was the same day that we found out she had been killed. I'm so sorry, but I was scared. And it was over, or so I thought."

"What do you mean?"

"They called again this morning. As soon as I answered, the voice said, 'Do not repeat your mistake again.' And the line went dead."

I tried comprehending all of this and asked, "How can you be sure that it's the same people? Why are you so convinced?"

She started crying. She said, "They killed my brother, Angelo."

CHAPTER 29

I HAD FINALLY GOTTEN Vanesa to calm down and stop crying. She was blaming herself for her brother's death and Lucy's. I got her back to Lewis's, and he was there waiting for us since I had texted him from our walk. He was ready with a coffee for Vanesa and some incense burning.

We sat around her, just being there for her until she was ready to talk. She sat up, took a deep breath, and said, "I'm ready."

I focused on her and said, "You told me your brother was killed in a car accident. Why do you think he was killed?"

"Somebody cut his brakes, so it wasn't an accident. The police report was filed as an accident, but the insurance said that the brake lines had been tampered with. When I called the police about it, they said to read the official report and that was their final decision on the matter," she said. "And it happened the day before Lucy was killed."

Lewis joined the conversation, "Angelo filled me in on what you had told him, but you said they called this morning, but didn't ask anything—just threatened you, right?"

"Yes, but it was the same voice, at least it sounded the same with the voice alteration," Vanesa explained.

Lewis then said, "OK, then they'll probably call again, and they will want something."

I jumped in, "You said that they wanted to know who your witness was before, so they will probably be wanting to find out about Camila now."

"But she's at the safe house, so even if they find out whose Vanesa's witness is, she won't be where they would be looking," Lewis stated.

"Right," I said. "But what if we give them a different location and we can be there waiting?"

"No! These are powerful people with professional hitmen," Vanesa cried out. "They made Lucy's death look like a home invasion and my brother's death look like an accident."

"No," I corrected her, "the police did that. I bet you if we pull the police report, it will tie back to one of our dirty detectives."

I continued, "If we set it up to happen in New Jersey, we can bring our FBI friends in, who we trust to at least bring down the person they hire to kill Camila. Because if it crosses state lines, it becomes an FBI case."

Lewis said, "I agree with you, Boss, but what if they don't try to kill her? What if they are sent there just to take her?"

"Either way, we catch someone trying to commit a crime. But you're right, so how 'bout we take this to Agent Grady Humble? See what he thinks and go with whatever plan he suggests. We already have Tanner working the detectives; let's work from another angle."

They both agreed, and Lewis made the call to Agent Humble.

CHAPTER 30

AGENT HUMBLE MADE SOME time for us after his shift and before he went home. He asked us to meet him at McGinty's, and of course, we were fine with that. Because it was after the afternoon rush but before the after-dinner crowd, we were able to talk privately at one of the back tables.

We all shook hands when Agent Humble arrived. I said, "Agent Grady Humble, this is Vanesa Galloway. She's a lawyer, and she has some details about some of the things we want to talk to you about. So, if you decide to help us, we can go over it later."

"Lewis, why do you always call me when you need help?" Grady was laughing as he said, "I thought we were just getting beers."

"I'm sorry, Grady," Lewis said. "I'll make sure my next call to you is a social one, but we do need your help."

"OK, let's hear it."

We started at the beginning, filling Agent Humble in with all the details so far. We told him about Detective Tanner and the dirty detectives. He was not a fan of Tanner's involvement but let us continue without much more discussion on his feelings about him. Then we told him about the phone calls to Vanesa, and how Lucy and Vanesa's brother both ended up being killed within two days of each other. Finally, we told him about the newest phone call and that we thought the person would be calling again for the new key witness and her whereabouts.

When we had finished, Grady stepped away from the table to call his wife and let her know he wouldn't be home for dinner. When he came back, he said, "All right, my wife isn't happy with me, but let's get some food ordered, and you all can tell me what you need me for."

When I went and ordered the food from Roy, he said, "Get in the back and make it. I know it's been a while since you've worked, but act like you know what you're doing, OK?"

I just laughed and jumped in the back to make our food. It's all deep-fried bar food, so it didn't take much to throw it all in the fryers. Roy didn't have any other customers at that time, but he liked giving me a hard time. But, on the flip side, he'd been very gracious to give me the time off, so I didn't mind at all.

I grabbed all the food and took it to our table. They all laughed and gave me a hard time because I had forgotten to take off the apron when I left the kitchen. Then they told me since I was on the clock to go grab another round for everyone. So, I did.

Finally, when we were finished eating, Grady said, "So?"

I started by saying, "We would like to set up the would-be killer," after a look from Lewis, I added, "or kidnapper, by giving them a location that we will have staked out. And we were wondering if we should do it in New Jersey, across the state line, so that the FBI would have jurisdiction."

"Well, I appreciate the thought, guys, and for another case to add to my load, but I don't think it would go the way you want." Grady continued, "If you get us involved, it will need to all be by the book and would take longer than you may want.

"So, my *off-the-record* advice is to handle it yourselves. I can help you with the strategy and setup, but I can't have any official link to it. We didn't have this conversation. I think you'll find you can set the trap quicker that way. And then when you're done with him, turn him over to the police. Say you saw him breaking into whatever location you sent him to and you made a citizen's arrest. If they turn him loose at that point, at least hopefully you will have the information you seek. Understand?"

Gazing steadily at Grady, Lewis said firmly, "Yes, thank you for buying us dinner for landing you the huge Grant Dogon case. You didn't have to, but thanks for arranging this evening for us."

Vanesa and I nodded in agreement that the previous conversation never happened. Agent Humble stood up, shook everyone's hand, and said, "Call me when we can talk again."

He went to the bar and paid for the tab for the night. Lewis, Vanesa, and I knew what we needed to do, so we headed home to be ready for the next day.

CHAPTER 31

I HAD LEWIS AND Vanesa drop me at my apartment. I wanted to be alone. I needed some time to think. Seeing Grady brought back memories of the last big case we worked on, Craig Mazer and Grant Dogon. I was also thinking of Cal Dunst and how he was killed for helping us. And now Nathan Grimble, who I think, whether or not we were involved, would have been pursuing the fire cases regardless.

So many lives had been taken, and for what? Can it all be to protect a multibillion-dollar pharmaceutical company from losing money on a drug that should have never been released in the first place? And unfortunately, the answer was probably yes because it always comes down to money.

I lay down, but I couldn't sleep. The thoughts running through my head were overwhelming. I couldn't even focus on one. The only thing I knew was that we needed to end the deaths that were piling up.

■ ■ ■

I must have eventually drifted off because I awoke to the sun shining through the window. My phone said it was 6:44 a.m.

I texted Joe and asked if he had time for breakfast, and he replied that he got off his 48-hour shift at 8 and could meet for a quick bite. I needed to catch him up on what had been going on and see what was being said about Grimble because I hadn't seen any stories in the news about it.

I asked Joe to meet me at Bluestone Lane Upper East Side, a great café with outdoor seating. They serve healthy breakfast items, but I go there for the cappuccino. It's right across from Central Park, so I can walk there.

I threw on my jogging clothes and decided I would get my workout in on the way to meet Joe. I was about halfway to the café when I got a phone call. It was Detective Tanner, and he wanted to meet. So, I told him I was meeting Joe for breakfast at Bluestone if he wanted to join us. He said he would see us there. I texted Joe that Tanner would be meeting with us as well.

I finished my run as I reached the Bluestone Café. I went in, got a cappuccino, and found a table outside. That's when I noticed the same blacked-out Lincoln Town Car that had been across the street from me when I stopped to take Tanner's call. I decided to approach the vehicle and try and figure out who was following me and why. Right when I started to cross the street in the car's direction, it peeled out and drove away. I had no idea who was inside, but I knew then that they knew I was involved in the Fibayson case. I needed to let everyone else know as well.

CHAPTER 32

I TEXTED TANNER TO just go home, and I'd explain why I couldn't meet later. I then texted Joe to stay at the fire station. I told him that I would meet him there as soon as I could. He didn't question it, just said OK. I then called Lewis to pick me up and to bring Vanesa with him. He said, "She already went to the law firm early this morning."

"OK, I'll call her. Just get here quickly, and watch for anyone following you. I'll explain more when you get here."

"Got it, Boss."

I called Vanesa, and when she answered, I asked, "Are you at work?"

She said, "Yes, and hello to you too."

"I'm sorry, hello, but we have a situation. I spotted someone following me, and I have no idea who it was. But they were definitely following me, because when I approached their vehicle, they sped off. Can you do your work from Lewis's?"

"Yes, let me gather some things, and I'll call for a ride from Lewis."

"Lewis is coming to pick me up. I'll have him send a car for you. If they're following me, they are probably following Lewis. They are most likely following you as well. I don't know about anyone else, and I don't want to talk about them over the phone, just in case. I'll see you later. Just answer when I call."

"OK, see you soon. Be careful, Angelo," she said softly before hanging up.

Right when I ended the call, Lewis pulled up. I got in the car, and he handed me two cell phones. He said, "I figured we might need these burner phones since you told me to watch for a tail. I've already programmed everyone's numbers into these phones. This is yours," as he pointed to the one in my right hand, "and the other one is for Joe. Now, turn off your old phone. I sent Vanesa's phone with the driver who is picking her up. He'll explain it to her. Now, what has got you so paranoid?"

I told him what happened, and he agreed with me that the three of us were probably being watched by someone. We needed to figure out if Tanner or Joe was being followed as well. And we decided to move Camila and her family and send additional protection, just in case. That would take some time, but we wanted to be sure that she didn't end up getting hurt.

We took a long and winding route to the firehouse, with both of us watching for a tail. After some time, we both felt safe that we were in the clear and went to the firehouse. We had the driver drop us off and park three blocks away and wait.

Joe was waiting for us right when we walked inside. He was visibly worried and said, "What's going on, Angelo? What's with the crazy meeting switch, and why here?"

"Joe, I was being followed when I went to the Bluestone Café. When I tried to confront the car, it drove off. We are assuming that if I am being followed, then Vanesa and Lewis are as well. But we don't know if you or Tanner have been connected with this yet. So, here is a burner phone. All our numbers are already in it. I need you to watch your back and check for tails."

"Awesome!" Joe said sarcastically. "So, what did you want to talk about?"

"Well, I wanted to catch you up on what has been going on. The long and the short of it is that Vanesa has gotten an anonymous phone call threatening her. She also received some back during Lucy's whistleblower case. They wanted to know who her witness was, and Vanesa wouldn't give in. They ended up killing her brother and eventually Lucy as well.

"So, Lewis and I have started planning, and we met with an FBI agent to discuss the situation and ask for help. Since we don't know who on the police we can trust outside of Detective Tanner, we reached out to someone we trust in the FBI to help with the legalities of what we want to do.

"That is the abbreviated version. But I also wanted to ask you about Grimble. What is the word around the firehouse?"

"No one really knows. The top brass are being very tight-lipped. All they know is that he is missing." Joe paused. "Or at least, that is all they will say to us. They've brought over a fire investigator from New Jersey to fill in until the truth comes out…which is very hard for me to not tell anyone."

"I understand, Joe, but we need to protect Detective Tanners cover until he can build his case on these guys. This is his case, and we wouldn't even know about the detectives' involvement if he hadn't told us, so it's our responsibility to keep it that way."

Joe said, "I know the danger it would put Detective Tanner in, so I will keep quiet. So, what do we do now?"

"Lewis, can you send a car for Joe? I want us to leave separately from him. Joe, stay here until Lewis's car comes, and we will all meet at the penthouse."

Lewis was looking at his phone when he realized I was talking to him. He looked up and said, "Yeah, I don't think that is going to work, Boss. My driver spotted a tail parked behind him. He moved to see if they would follow, and he drove by the fire station and said that there was another car sitting outside as well. I just told him to drive all around the city until his shift ends or they stop following and to go home. We need another plan."

With a little excitement on his face, Joe said, "I have an idea. I'll be right back."

CHAPTER 33

JOE RETURNED TO WHERE he'd left us standing, bringing his captain with him. Captain Lamke said, "So, I hear you guys want a ride in one of our rigs? Lucky for you guys, I just got one back from the shop and it isn't registered back in service yet, so I can take you for a ride. You ready?"

Lewis said, "Yes, sir. Thanks so much for taking us for a ride on such short notice."

"Yes, thank you," I said. "We were telling Joe how we always wanted to go for a ride-along, and he said he would go ask. And we need a ride to Lewis's, which is only a couple blocks away. Can you drop us there?"

Captain Lamke said, "That shouldn't be a problem. But I do want to warn you that if a major emergency gets called in, I'll have to come back here."

"We understand. If that happens, you could drop us in the middle of the street. We just appreciate the chance to ride in a real fire truck, even for a short ride," I said.

We pulled out of the fire station with the sirens going, only to avoid the busy intersection. The captain drove, Joe was in the passenger seat, and Lewis and I were in the back seats. There were so many safety straps to be buckled into, and there were compartments everywhere. We couldn't be sure that the truck wasn't being followed, but we highly doubted it. It would probably take them a while to realize we were gone.

About a block and a half into the ride, Captain Lamke came over the headsets he had given us to wear. He said, "Sorry, guys, but I hope you're OK walking the rest of the way. We just had a car bombing a couple blocks away from the station. Luckily there were no casualties, but I need to be there and figure out what the hell is going on. Rain check?"

"Of course, Captain, thanks for taking my brother for a quick ride," Joe said. "Hopefully it will keep him off my back about a ride-along for a little bit. Stay safe."

We all hopped out, and Captain Lamke hit the sirens and went flying back the way we had come. At that same moment, Lewis's phone rang. He answered, and from his face, it was not a pleasant conversation.

When he hung up, he said, "Well, the car that blew up was mine. The caller was using my driver's phone and said that this was a warning. Next time, someone will get hurt. He told me that we need to stay away from the lawyer's case, and he ended the call."

"Well, at least no one got hurt, but we are not staying away," I said angrily. "We just need to be more cautious. We probably need to put Vanesa in a safe house and keep our distance from being seen with her. We need to move ahead quickly and quietly. Lewis, can you please set that up?"

"Got it, but I need to go take care of my driver and insurance. I'll make some calls as I walk over there. You guys head to my place and wait for me there. We'll sort this out, Boss."

"Hey, Lewis, be careful. I'm sure they'll be watching but shouldn't do anything with so many eyes around. Just get back safely so we can see this through."

CHAPTER 34

JOE AND I MADE the short walk to Lewis's while watching all the emergency response services passing us on their way to the bombing. We didn't say much on the walk back. I was still processing what was happening. I had never been threatened like this before.

As we walked to the front of the building, the doorman and desk attendant were standing outside watching all the commotion. The deskman asked, "Where is Mr. Pollard? He phoned earlier and said the three of you were on your way. Miss Galloway is already here."

"He's handling a situation. He'll be here in a little while," I said.

Pointing in the direction of a plume of smoke coming from a few blocks away, the doorman asked, "What's going on over there?"

"We heard there was a car fire or something. Not really sure," Joe said, as we headed toward the elevator.

Vanesa was waiting for us when the elevator doors opened. She asked, "What's going on? Where's Lewis?"

"We'll get to where Lewis is in a minute," I said. "But whoever is threatening you is following us as well. At least Lewis and me.

We're unsure whether they know if Joe or Detective Tanner are involved yet. That is why you should now have a burner phone, and we are going to have to move you. You'll need to be in a safe house and somehow do your work from there."

Vanesa, worried now, asked, "How will I still work on the case with you guys? How can I do my job on the lawsuit being away from my office?"

"For now, you'll need to be behind the scenes. We will still communicate with you daily, but we want you to be safe. This will hopefully be solved soon, and we can all go back to our normal, crazy lives.

"As for Lewis, his car was just bombed as a warning to us. This is why we are taking your safety into consideration. These guys obviously are willing to kill to keep us away from finding out the truth, whatever it may be."

"Did anyone get hurt?" Vanesa asked, shocked and getting more upset by the minute.

Joe said, "We don't know for sure. We know Lewis's driver is OK, and we don't believe there were any casualties, but injuries probably did occur."

"Right, we don't know, but Lewis is over there now helping figure it out and taking care of his driver and the car," I said. "Again, we all must be very cautious. Have they called you yet to find out who your witness is?"

"No, they haven't called again," Vanesa replied.

"OK, well, they probably will be soon, and we will figure out how to handle it before it happens. For now, though, get your things packed up as we all wait for Lewis to get back."

Vanesa begrudgingly went to her room to get her personal belongings. Joe looked worriedly at me and asked, "Is my son safe? Do I need to warn them?"

"I can't answer that with a guarantee, but I know that Lewis will make some calls to have your family protected, Joe. We will take care of this."

CHAPTER 35

WHEN THE ELEVATOR PINGED, four heads turned to stare at Lewis coming through the doors. I had reached out to Detective Tanner while we were waiting for Lewis and had him come to be here when Lewis got back.

Lewis looked very disheveled. Normally his clothes were perfectly fit, nothing out of place. But right then, Lewis was a mess. His shirt was torn, and he had soot all over himself. He actually looked like he was the one in the car bombing.

He wearily regarded all of us and said, "I need a shower first. I'll have my chef prepare some food, then we can talk. We have a lot to discuss. I'm glad you're here, Tanner. We're going to need your help."

We all just nodded our heads and watched as Lewis slowly made his way to the kitchen and back out to his bedroom. We sat in silence as we waited.

Eventually Lewis came out looking like a magazine cover model. The chef was one step behind him with plates for all of us. Lewis said, "Everyone, please start eating. While we nourish our bodies, be thankful for the life we have and never take all our friendships for granted. I love each and every one of you… even you, Tanner. So, let's eat, and then we can talk."

Chef Emilio never disappoints. He usually cooks for one or two people, but at the drop of a hat, he had prepared five gourmet lunches for us. The crispy pork and grilled asparagus were so harmonious with each other. He even gave us a small gelato cup to finish up. It tasted like he made it, and he probably did.

When everyone had finished and put their napkins on top of their plate, Vanesa and I cleared the table. While we were in the kitchen, she asked, "Is Lewis OK?"

I said, "I'm not totally sure. I have never seen him like that. Let's go find out."

As we walked back into the room, everyone was seated in the living room. Lewis said, "First, I want you all to know that I am a little shocked by this whole situation. Those who know me well know that I am usually the one that is a step ahead. But right now, I feel two steps behind these people. Thankfully, no one was critically injured or killed, but they made it very apparent it could go that way if necessary.

"The next part makes me just as uneasy. Detective Grims was the lead on the 'accidental car fire' case," Lewis emphasized with air quotes.

Detective Tanner quickly said, "That doesn't make any sense. He's a homicide detective, and he's supposed to be off today!"

"Right," Lewis said. "He introduced himself to me as Homicide Detective Grims. And when I questioned why he was handling the case when there was no homicide, he quickly dismissed me and said everyone else was too busy for a small car fire."

Lewis continued, "Now, obviously, I recognized the name immediately, but I didn't show my hand. But it also means that these detectives of yours, Tanner, are working with the people following us because he was first on scene. He made it very clear to the firefighters and Captain Lamke that they were there just to put out the fire and that this was his case. He even went on to say that this wasn't even really a case but an accidental car fire, and he just needed to get this piece of junk off the congested streets.

"He didn't even question me or my driver. Just gave us the number to the impound lot in case we wanted to get the wreck back or for insurance. He also handed me a copy of his report that he said I could use to turn in to insurance stating it was deemed an accident."

I took my chance to speak up and said, "But, Lewis, why were you covered in soot and your clothes all ripped up? I thought maybe another bomb had gone off or something when you got there."

"No, no, Boss," Lewis said, shaking his head. "As soon as the fire was out, I tried getting under the car while Grims was talking to the tow truck driver. I wanted to see if I could get anything to prove that it was a bomb and not an accident. But Grims noticed me and ran over and pulled me out from under there. He was yelling that this was a crime scene, and I couldn't be near the vehicle.

"Holding up the report he had just given me, I reminded him it was just an accident. He quickly caught himself and said he was just trying to keep everyone safe, and there may still be a fire burning under there. That he couldn't have anyone dying under his watch. I decided to let it go and walked here. I sent my driver home in a taxi, and that's that."

Detective Tanner said, "You may as well throw that impound number away. I have a good feeling that when you call, they'll say the car was never brought there, and then you'll get the runaround from the department. That car is headed straight to a compactor."

"I figured that out already, but thanks for the confirmation," Lewis said.

Lewis stood up and walked over to the countertop. He grabbed something from it and said, "I did manage to grab this from the bottom of the car before Grims pulled me out!"

CHAPTER 36

LEWIS WAS HOLDING A small device. He said that it was the detonator, or at least a part of one. I asked, "Do you think we can get prints off of it?"

"I hope so, Boss," Lewis said. "But we will need to call in a few favors to get it done. I don't think we can trust the police lab right now."

Vanesa joined in the conversation and said, "I have a friend who could do it. She can pull the prints for us, and then she has someone that can run it through the database. Let me give her a call."

Vanesa strolled into the other room, already dialing a number. Detective Tanner joined Lewis to inspect the piece of metal he was holding. Lewis said, "Do you know anything about bombs, Tanner?"

"Not much," Detective Tanner said as he turned it over in his hands. "It looks like a remote start detonator though. I can't tell if it's a cell phone–activated one or a push button though."

I asked, "Does it matter which it is?"

Tanner looked back at me and said, "Well, not technically. It's still a bomb, and that's not great. But, if it were a cell phone–activated one, those are higher tech and take longer to build. A push-button remote is much simpler bomb technology. All that to say, depending on which it is could tell us how advanced these people are. The more advanced means more money and funding behind all of this. Remember, always follow the money."

"OK, so is there a way to figure it out?"

"I'm not sure, but I'll take a picture of it and ask someone I trust on the bomb squad."

Detective Tanner took a picture and headed toward the elevator. I asked, "Where are you going?"

"I'm going to head to work and see what, if anything, Grims will say to me about the 'car fire' case. I'll call you later on the burner phone, Angelo."

"Be cautious, Tanner. We don't know who is watching yet, and you are working with some bad dudes, who could make you disappear in an instant," I said as the elevator doors closed.

Just then, Vanesa came back in and said that her friend would take care of it. She would need Lewis to bring it down to her at her office because she would need to get his prints as well to eliminate them when they hopefully find prints on the device. I told Joe to go home and maybe find a friend's place where he could lay low for a few days. He said he would, but that he was going to stop by the firehouse and make sure Captain Lamke didn't need any help after the car bombing.

CHAPTER 37

LEWIS, VANESA, AND I headed down to Precision Forensics. Vanesa's friend, Dana Cochran, was the owner. Precision Forensics, I found out, does consulting work for police departments that are either overloaded or don't have their own forensics labs.

When we pulled up, it was to a nondescript concrete block building. There was no signage or anything that would show there was anything inside the building. Even on the door, the only sign read, "Please Ring Bell for Service." So, we rang the bell, and a voice came over an intercom that I couldn't even see and said, "Name of person you are here to see?"

Vanesa said, "I'm Vanesa Galloway here to see Dana. She's expecting me."

There was no response, but a buzzer sounded, and we were able to open the door. We walked through the vestibule and discovered state-of-the-art equipment from wall to wall. A woman who looked to be the same age as Vanesa came toward us. Her walk commanded respect. You could tell right away that she was the person who ran things and did it well. I assumed this was Dana, and I was right. Vanesa introduced me and Lewis, and we all shook hands. Even her handshake conveyed strength.

"How can I help you all? Vanesa didn't really tell me what was going on, but if she calls, I know that it's important and urgent," Dana said.

Lewis held up the detonator that was now in a baggie. He said, "Someone blew up one of my cars, and I was able to recover part of the detonator. We were hoping that maybe you could find fingerprints or DNA or anything that could help us."

"Is everyone OK?" she asked with genuine concern.

I said, "Yes, thankfully, everyone is OK. But I'm sure since we are here and not at the police station, you understand that this is strictly confidential. The detective in charge deemed it a car fire and an accident. He is protecting someone, and we need to figure out who. We cannot trust the police."

Dana laughed a little and said, "I wouldn't trust them with anything. I've learned my lesson the hard way. And anything I do is strictly confidential; no worries there. Can I have that?" she asked as she reached for the baggie, and Lewis handed it to her. "Let me take this over to my techs and tell them what to get started on, then we can meet in my office. It's in the far-right corner. I'll be there soon."

Dana walked in one direction, and we headed to the far-right corner of the building. I noticed that as she began talking to two techs, they listened intently to her every word. Whatever she asked of them, they were going to get it done immediately.

We sat waiting in Dana's office for only a few minutes when she came in. She said, "OK, that's started. I can't guarantee the results because I don't know what's on there. Also, Lewis, I need you to go just outside my office where a tech will be waiting for you. We need a sample of your DNA and your fingerprints to rule them out if we find anything."

After Lewis left the room, Dana continued, "Vanesa, what have you gotten me into?"

Vanesa went through the entire story with my input here and there, up until where we were today. Dana didn't seem worried or scared at all by the situation. She simply said, "I will do my best. And if you need anything else, I'll be here to help."

We collected Lewis as Dana walked us out. She shook my hand and Lewis's and gave Vanesa a hug. She said, "Give me a day or two. I'll be in touch. And, Vanesa, don't be a stranger."

CHAPTER 38

OVER THE NEXT TWO days, we waited. We were still doing everything we could to keep everyone out of harm's way while we waited for the results from the lab and for the mysterious caller to make contact with Vanesa again.

During that time, we found a new safe house for Camila and her family, while stationing Lewis's guys at the old safe house for when the call came. We had also secured a new location for Vanesa for the time being. We gave her the burner phone while keeping her original phone with us. Any call that came through was forwarded to her burner, but we also were on the other end of the line to be ready for the caller with the altered voice.

On the second day Dana from Precision Forensics called Vanesa. Vanesa connected us to the call. Dana said, "We have found something, but it doesn't make sense to us, and I'd rather you all came back here to discuss."

We agreed, and Lewis sent a car to pick up Vanesa so we could all meet at Precision. This time when we pressed the button, the door opened immediately. No questions, no delay. Dana was standing in the middle of the floor waiting for us. She said, "Let's go to my office."

Once we were all inside, she shut the door. She started by saying, "Listen, this was a very strange situation here. First, I want to tell you that we did find some things out, but there are some disturbing things surrounding all of it. Let's begin with the detonator itself. It was not the detonator used in this bombing. I say this because all the switch work and mechanisms are still intact and have not been fired. It also had very little damage on it from the bomb itself. I believe that they planted it there so that you would find it, and it must have had some kind of blast cap on it protecting it and keeping it intact. So, that's the first strange thing.

"Next, we did find some fingerprints. Obviously, we found yours, Lewis, as expected. The next set of fingerprints we found on the detonator was something altogether unexpected, but I'd like to come back to that. What we then found, and what they probably didn't expect us to find, was a partial print on the inside of the detonator on the back of the metal plate. We were able to match those partials to two possible suspects, and we ruled one of them out because that person has been out of the country for the past five years. So, we were left with one possible suspect, and his name is Hank Dupont. The little bit of information we found on Mr. Dupont is that he was arrested and charged for making and selling fertilizer bombs out of his storage unit. He served ten years and had gotten out just over three years ago. Here is his latest known address," she said, handing Vanesa a sheet with a New York address.

"And finally, back to the other fingerprint found on the detonator casing. This may be difficult to hear, and we think that it was put there to send a message to you, Mr. Barsotti."

"To me? Why me? It was Lewis's car they bombed," I said, rather distressed.

Dana continued, "Well, the print belonged to Lucy Barsotti."

CHAPTER 39

LUCY FLOODED MY MIND again, and all I could see was us on our wedding day. Everything was blurry, but I knew where we were. The only thing that was clear was our hands. I was holding Lucy's hand as I slid the ring on her finger. And my memory froze there, with her hand in mine. I snapped out of it and said, "How?"

I was calmer than I expected, and I was focused on the answer from Dana. She said, "There are many ways that they could have gotten her fingerprints, but they must have been holding onto it for the last few years or they were able to duplicate her prints using some advanced technology. The reason I said they had put it there was because it was a transferred fingerprint. It was not made by someone touching the object. There were no oils or DNA transferred onto the device."

"OK, so we need to focus on Hank Dupont. We can't worry about the fact that they are trying to intimidate us. If we waste time focusing on the wrong things, we won't get to the bottom of all this." I continued, "How far away is the last known address for Mr. Dupont?"

Lewis said, "I already have people en route to search the place, but we can head that way too. With traffic, we can probably be there in twenty minutes."

▪ ▪ ▪

When we pulled up to the place of Dupont's last known address, it was a run-down house that looked like it hadn't been taken care of for many years. After Lewis talked to his guys, he came back and said, "They searched the area around the property but didn't try to approach the door. They said they haven't seen any activity since they arrived."

"OK," I said. "Let's see if anyone is home."

Vanesa asked, "Are you just going to knock on the front door?"

"It seems like the best approach," I said as we marched up to the door.

As soon as we reached the top of the steps, a man came from the back of the house. He was very calm but said, "I have the entire place wired and ready to blow. All I have to do is make the call and…BOOM!

"Now, who are you and what do you want?"

"Are you Hank Dupont?" I asked. "We just want to talk."

"Maybe I am and maybe I'm not. What do you want to talk about?"

I started walking toward the man, but he said, "Stay where you are, or we all become part of the blast."

Right as he finished saying that, one of Lewis's guys tackled him from behind, knocking the phone from his hand. I ran over, grabbed the phone, and smashed it on the ground. I asked him again, "Are you Hank Dupont?"

"What does it matter?" He said, "You're just going to take me back to jail!"

"We are not the police, but we can call them if you'd like. Or," I offered, "you can talk to us."

"If I talk, they'll kill me."

Lewis asked, "Who are they?"

Mr. Dupont looked around, scared now. It seemed like he would rather us have been the police. I asked him again, "Who are they, Hank?"

Finally, Hank responded, "Fine! Fine! I'll talk. But we need to leave now. Whoever you are, if you found me, they're probably not far behind."

CHAPTER 40

ONCE WE WERE ALL loaded into Lewis's car, Lewis decided that Precision Forensics was closer and probably safer than his apartment. Vanesa called Dana, and she said that it would be OK to come there. Lewis had his guys stay and search Mr. Dupont's house and shed. We verified with Mr. Dupont that there would be no explosives going off, and he reluctantly told us that it was safe.

Lewis had his driver take a crazy route back to Precision, looking for tails the entire way. We didn't notice anyone, so that was a win for us. We entered the lab and went straight back to Dana's office. Dana left the room after we were all seated.

"OK, Hank…can I call you Hank?" He nodded, and I continued, "We know that you are a bomb maker. But who are you working for?"

Hank said, "I don't work for anyone, not exclusively. I get hired by job. I make whatever is called for. But…" His voice trailed off.

Vanesa pleaded with him, "But what, Hank? I can understand what you're going through. I have been threatened by possibly the same people. So, who has you so scared? We need to find them before anyone else gets hurt!"

"But if they threatened you, how are you still alive? Did you do whatever they told you to do?"

Vanesa said, "No, I didn't, but they killed someone close to me instead. So again, I know you are frightened, but we could save others."

Hank rubbed his face and eyes and then said, "I don't have a name, but I think I have a theory on who I was working for. They hired me to make six bombs. They wanted three smaller ones for car bombs, and three larger ones to bomb buildings. They told me to make them do minimal damage but enough to leave a mark. I wasn't used to this because people who usually hire me want bombs that do maximum damage. But they said that they wanted a controlled scenario, so I did it.

"Then the next strange thing happened. The people who called for the bombs were not the ones who picked them up. They called and said that four detectives would be picking them up. At first, I thought I had been set up and they were coming to arrest me, but when they showed up, they inspected all the bombs and discussed what each one was for. They tried being quiet, but I heard them. As they left, they warned me that if I even thought about talking, then they could make me disappear and no one would find my body."

Vanesa, Lewis, and I shared a knowing look. I said, "Did you get the detectives' names?"

Hank laughed a little and said, "No. They didn't offer that information, and after their warning, I didn't say a word."

Since Detective Tanner wasn't there, we didn't know what the dirty detectives looked like, except for Grims. Lewis gave a detailed description of Grims to Hank. Hank said, "Yeah, that sounds like one of them. That was the short one, I think."

Now we had a second connection between the detectives and the guys following us. *But who are they all working for?* I said, "Wait! Didn't you say you thought you knew who it was that hired you?"

Hank grinned and said, "I said I have a theory."

CHAPTER 41

WE ALL WAITED FOR him to say more. Finally, Lewis, exasperated, prompted, "Well, what's your theory?"

Hank, who'd been staring at me, said, "I know who you are. You're Angelo Barsotti."

I didn't really know what to do with that, so I said, "OK, what does that have to do with anything?"

"I always wondered what was going on." Hank more talking to himself than us, continued, "I didn't understand why we had to do what we did. I never created something for a bomb that WASN'T supposed to blow up. And I really didn't understand why I had to plant prints on it. Is that how you found me?"

I was getting tired of this. "Hank, who hired you or what's your theory?" I asked sharply.

Hank continued rambling, "Did I leave some trace of my fingerprints on that piece? I swear I wiped it down. But I guess I was being too careful not erasing your wife's prints from the detonator."

Vanesa yelled, a little too loudly, "Hank! Why did you put the prints there?"

Hank finally made eye contact with me and said, "They told me to. They said that if I wasn't successful with this task that I wouldn't be paid for any of it."

Again, I asked, "Who are 'they'? What are you going on about?"

"Ok, OK, OK. If you follow the bombs that I made and you know some of what I know, you could figure out a theory as well. But since you do not know what I know, I'll tell you. I made two small bombs that they told me would be put into filing cabinets. They wanted the explosions to be small enough to destroy the cabinet and anything in it, but only to cause a fire after going off. So, when I saw the research facilities that caught on fire, I figured out those were my bombs. I know what they said that it was an electrical fire, but I knew better. It's too much of a coincidence for two facilities owned by the same company to both accidentally catch fire within one week of each other.

"They also had me make three car bombs, not big enough to destroy a car, but enough to do damage. They said that the fake detonator needed to look exactly like the car bomb detonators and have the prints on it. They also made me build a blast cap to protect it. But they wanted two of the bombs to be duds. They wanted them to be completely active bombs, but with the switch disabled, so they wouldn't go off.

"When the detectives picked them up, they needed to know which ones were which. After I handed them each bomb and told them, they began discussing among themselves and I over-heard the names Mayor Daniels, Byron Mitchell (who I've never heard of), and Lewis Pollard. That's you, right?"

He was looking right at Lewis. He said, "Did they bomb your car?"

Lewis shook his head and said, "We are the ones with the questions, not you. Understand?" Hank just nodded. Lewis continued, "That guy, Byron Mitchell, he's the president of Fibayson."

Vanesa said, "Yeah, that's him. He is the named person in the class action lawsuit against Fibayson."

The three of us stepped out of Dana's office. I said to Lewis and Vanesa, "If the real bomb was used on you, Lewis, that means that the duds are meant for Mayor Daniels and Byron Mitchell."

Vanesa asked, "Why would they plant dud bombs?"

"They want it to look like an attack on Fibayson," I said. "But what I don't get is how is Mayor Daniels involved?"

CHAPTER 42

WHILE WE WERE STILL outside Dana's office, Lewis told us that his guys had found all kinds of bomb-making equipment in Hank Dupont's shed. We made a not-so-anonymous call to FBI Agent Grady Humble about the shed and where they could find Mr. Dupont.

We just let Hank Dupont sit in Dana's office while we worked out what to do next. Within an hour, Agent Hicks, Humble's partner, was at the facility. When he walked in, he nodded at Lewis and me and said, "I heard you caught another one for us. Thanks for giving Grady the heads-up. Getting a bomber off the streets is a win for the FBI."

"No problem," Lewis said. "One of his bombs blew up one of my cars, so I'm glad you'll be taking care of him."

I opened the door to Dana's office and let Agent Hicks in. He immediately announced who he was and why he was there. Mr. Dupont instantly froze and went wide-eyed. He started yelling, "I told you guys what you wanted! You said you wouldn't call the cops!"

Agent Hicks smiled and said, "They didn't, sir. They called the FBI, and I promise you, we are *not* the cops."

After all the commotion, we thanked Dana for her help. She said to call if we needed anything else. I told Lewis to start digging deeper into Fibayson and to begin a deep dive into Mayor Daniels. He said it would be difficult, but he would get right on it. Just as we stepped outside, my phone rang from a blocked number.

I answered, "Hello?"

The voice on the other end was distorted, and it said, "Why did you get Mr. Dupont involved? And then have him arrested? Now I'm going to have to clean up the mess you created. If you don't want to end up like Mr. Dupont, the next time I call, you will give me answers to whatever I ask. I have now given you, Mr. Pollard, and Miss Galloway warnings. I will not warn you again."

The call ended.

Lewis noticed my face had darkened and queried, "Who was that?"

I said, "It was the caller. Probably the one who threatened Vanesa and also called you after your car was bombed. He now says that we have all been warned, and if we don't comply with his next instructions, then we will end up like Mr. Dupont."

Vanesa asked, "Arrested? For what?"

"I don't think that's what is going to happen to Mr. Dupont. The caller has a plan for him that I don't think will be good. We can try and warn Agents Humble and Hicks, but…"

Lewis prodded, "But what, Boss?"

"How did he know that Hank Dupont was arrested already? Apparently, we are dealing with someone very powerful, who has their hands in a lot of different pockets. We need to be quick and figure out who…before someone else gets hurt."

CHAPTER 43

I AWOKE THE NEXT morning with Lewis standing over me. I had stayed at his place for security reasons, but we had sent Vanesa back to her safe house. I rubbed my eyes and asked, "What time is it? What's going on?"

Lewis looked upset. He said, "Hank Dupont is dead. Agent Humble is in the hospital but is OK. Another person in FBI holding is dead as well."

I sat straight up, "WHAT!?"

Lewis continued, "There was a bombing at the New York City FBI Office. They blew up exactly where Hank Dupont was being held, and Grady happened to be nearby. He's being treated for minor injuries and is expected to make a full recovery. But this is serious, Boss. They were able to kill Hank Dupont in FBI custody and knew his exact location in the building where he was being held."

"You're right, Lewis, this is not good. We now know that they have insiders on the police and FBI. We are going to have to stop this on our own before anyone else is killed. Let's go see Grady in the hospital and see if he can tell us anything."

"OK, Boss. I will send for a car. Get ready to leave in five. I also have added protection for Vanesa, Joe, and Joe's son."

"Thank you, Lewis. I'll be out in a few."

■ ■ ■

We arrived at the hospital, where the smell of disinfectant hung in the air. We found where Grady was being treated. An agent was stationed outside his room, but he allowed us in. Lewis walked over to him and said, "You good, bud?"

Grady said, "Yeah, I'll be fine. I'm getting out of here in the next hour or so."

I said, "That's great to hear. I'm sorry we brought this mess to your doorstep, and we already have plans to clean it up."

"Oh no, you don't!" Grady said very sternly. "They attacked an FBI field office! We will be hunting them down! You both need to stay out of it now."

"But we know how to handle—"

Lewis cut me off. "You've got it, Agent Humble. We'll step back."

I gave Lewis a look, but he just shook his head. He then said, "Well, we just wanted to check on you, old friend. We'll let you get out of here and start your manhunt."

I said, "Yeah…glad to see you're OK, Grady."

We left the room, walking down the sterile hallway lined with dingy white floor tiles. Once we were out of earshot, I exploded, "What was that, Lewis? Why did you say we were just going to drop this?"

"I know, Boss, but don't worry. Grady gave me a look. We aren't out of this at all. But he had to make it clear that he told us we were no longer to investigate. He'll call us when he gets out. We will still have cooperation from him. Maybe not the whole FBI, but Grady will keep us in the loop."

CHAPTER 44

IT DIDN'T TAKE LONG. Grady called Lewis two hours later. Lewis put the call on speaker as Grady was saying, "Look, guys, this is not a good situation. Also, I don't know who I can trust inside my own unit now because they got to Hank Dupont inside his holding cell. They almost got me killed. So, I cannot work directly with you as an FBI agent, but I'll help any way I can as a friend and someone you can trust. I must go now, but I'll call back as soon as I know more. I'm headed to the office now for a debriefing."

As soon as Lewis hung up the phone, I asked, "What do you have on Mayor Daniels? While we wait on Grady, we need to follow our leads."

"We're looking into his connections with Fibayson and the police department. We have just added any connections to the FBI as well. Let me make a call and see if they have anything new since last night."

As Lewis made his phone call, I made one of my own. When the person on the other end picked up, I said, "Hello, is Mayor Daniels in today? … No, that's OK, I don't need an appointment. Thank you."

Lewis gave me a confused look. I just told him to ask one of his drivers to take us to city hall; Mayor Daniels was in his office today. As soon as he hung up with his people, he called the driver. We headed down to wait. When we stepped into the elevator, Lewis asked, "Are you going to fill me in on what we're doing?"

"We're just going to have a talk with our mayor," I explained. "We are his constituents, and I have some questions for him."

Lewis looked perplexed. "We can't just walk in there and expect him to see us."

"I know, Lewis, but if he is involved in all this, then he knows who we are. Either he'll see us or he'll have us escorted out. Then we'll at least have some clarity on who knows what."

When the car pulled up, we got in. Lewis countered, "But—"

I got a phone call from Joe. I showed Lewis the phone as I answered. "Hey, Joe, you're on speaker with me and Lewis."

"Hey, guys, just wanted to let you know that they finally have filed a missing persons case for Grimble. Can't we get involved now?"

I said, "Not yet, Joe. It won't change anything. Better that you stay out of it for now. We don't want to let them know that we know."

Dejectedly, Joe said, "OK, Angelo, I understand."

After we hung up, Lewis asked, "What are we going to say to Mayor Daniels? What if he just refuses to see us?"

"Just follow my lead."

"Got it, Boss."

CHAPTER 45

WHEN WE ARRIVED AT New York City Hall, the driver dropped us off at the portico. New York City Hall looks like a grander version of the White House. The national landmark, still as impressive as when it was built in 1812, houses New York City officials, including the mayor.

We followed the signs to Mayor Daniels' offices. A receptionist sat at a desk right where we entered. He asked, "How may I help you today?"

I replied, "I'm Angelo Barsotti, private investigator, and this is my associate, Lewis Pollard. We would like to speak to Mayor Daniels."

The receptionist said, "I don't see an appointment for you on the books today. I apologize, but the mayor is a very busy man. You can either leave a note with me and I'll see what we can get on the schedule, or you are welcome to wait and see if any free time comes up. But I would suggest the note option, as the mayor usually has no free time."

He seemed very friendly and probably dealt with similar situations all day. But I said, "If you could just let him know we're here, we will wait."

"He's in a meeting, but I will send a message through our interoffice messaging and let him know. Please have a seat over there to wait."

Just as Lewis and I were about to sit down, Mayor Daniels walked out of his office. He said, "Mr. Barsotti, Mr. Pollard, I am in a meeting, but apparently you know who I'm meeting with, so please come in."

Lewis and I shared a look of confusion, but we decided to take advantage of the opportunity. We followed Mayor Daniels into his office. When we saw who was there, our confusion went to another level. Standing there smiling was…Vanesa.

She said, "Hey, guys. I'm sure you're wondering why I'm here. But it's probably the same reason you are. So, I asked the mayor to have you join us."

"Yes, Miss Galloway here was just asking me about bombs and about that person who was killed in FBI custody," Mayor Daniels said. "We only started a few minutes ago, but I've already told Miss Galloway I have no idea what she is talking about. Of course, I know about Hank Dupont; my security team debriefed me this morning. But as far as a bomb or bomb threat, I have no idea. Also, I had never heard of Hank Dupont before this morning. So, unless there is anything else, I really must get back to serving the city."

I was still in state of shock, but I managed to say, "We talked to Mr. Dupont, Mayor Daniels. Mr. Dupont is a well-documented bomb maker, and he specifically mentioned your name. He said that the people who picked up the bombs from him said that they were going to plant a fake bomb on one of your vehicles. You have no knowledge of this at all?"

"I have no knowledge of this. I haven't had a threat of any bombs in the first three years of my term, let alone a fake one,"

Mayor Daniels said. "Look, I'm really sorry you came all the way here, but I really must get back to it. Graham will validate your parking on your way out. And Miss Galloway left her phone number with me already. If something comes up, I'll be sure to call. Thank you."

He led us out the door, and as soon as we were out, he closed it behind us. None of us needed validation, so instead, I left my card with Graham, just in case.

I turned my attention to Vanesa. "What are you doing here?"

She looked at me like I was dumb and said, "I was simply following leads, like you two."

"But Vanesa, we have you moved to another location for a reason. It isn't safe right now. We need to be watching out for everyone."

Lewis said, "Yes, Vanesa, please let us do this part of the case. We need you working on the legal side of things and not being out where someone could get to you."

Vanesa said, "I have your people with me, Lewis. One is waiting just outside, and the other is in the car waiting to pick us up. I am being safe."

I said, "I know that you want to help with all of this, but we need to limit the people who are involved, and we need you nailing down the class action. Please, stay in your safe house or the office. It won't be long now, but until then, can you promise to do that?"

"Fine, Angelo, but I don't like being in hiding. I spent the last few months running from these people, and I don't want that life anymore. Keep me in the loop please, so at least I can help from where I am."

With that she left us standing at the front of the building, collected her protection, and got in the car with one of Lewis's drivers.

CHAPTER 46

BACK IN ONE OF Lewis's cars, we headed back to his place, unsure where else to go at this point. I decided to call Detective Tanner and see where he was on the dirty detectives.

"Hey, Angelo, how's everything going with the bombings? I heard about the FBI holding cells being blown up. Was that one of the guys you were chasing down?"

I said, "They blew up the guy who was responsible for making the bombs. Tying up loose ends, I guess. Where are you at with the detectives? Any closer to getting them off the streets and being able to interrogate them?"

"We were. We had been meeting with the district attorney—behind closed doors, of course—and then we were told to stand down. Apparently, the mayor's office got wind of it and shut down the entire investigation."

"The mayor's office or the mayor himself?" I asked.

"I'm not sure. We weren't given any more than that. But as soon as we heard they were shutting us down, we started making copies of everything. Within hours, a courier came from the mayor's office to collect anything involving the investigation."

I asked, "What does your commander have to say about all of it?"

"What can he say? Of course, he fought back, but at the end of the day, he has to do what the mayor says."

"I get it. So, what's the plan now?"

Tanner said, "I'm on my way to Lewis's with copies of everything. My commander said we have no official investigation going but that I could help you try and figure this out. And then maybe we'll be able to get these guys anyway. But I must stay off the streets. Once the detectives find out who I really was, I could be in danger."

"We have your back. And Tanner…thank you. We'll see you soon."

CHAPTER 47

WE HAD ARRIVED BACK to Lewis's, but on the ride, Lewis had gotten a phone call from his "sources." They had tracked multiple large donations to Mayor Daniels' campaign from Fibayson. They had made multiple injections of funds at the beginning of Mayor Daniels' initial push for the mayor's seat and were funding him once again on his reelection campaign. There was also a mysterious offshore account that had multiple transactions, but Lewis's people hadn't tracked who was receiving these funds yet, who owned it, or who else had access to the account.

Now we had a link between Fibayson and Mayor Daniels, and from Mayor Daniels to the dirty detectives, since the mayor's office shut down the investigation into the detectives. We just needed to figure out the end game of all of this and how Lucy's murder was connected. Obviously, it all comes down to money, but why?

Detective Tanner was waiting inside the penthouse. He had four boxes full of documents dealing with the dirty detectives. He said, "Of course you just got here! I just finished lugging all this up here by myself!"

I said, "Sorry. Lewis received some information tying Fibayson to Mayor Daniels and his campaign funding."

"And Mayor Daniels just shut down our case," Tanner said.

"Right, so now we need to figure out how they all fit together. We need to see if there's a tie between Mayor Daniels and the money going to the detectives. You know they are getting paid for each job they cover up, but we need to prove where it came from."

Tanner said, "That will be a hard one to trace. It's always cash. And the money they've paid me on the jobs for my cut was always logged into IA evidence and wasn't traceable—meaning it hadn't been stolen or 'dirty' money—to any specific location. Trust me, we've been working on that since I made it into their group."

I glanced at Lewis. "I have an idea. Can you get Keith on the phone and see if he has time to help us? We won't need him to fly out for this one, but we will need his hacking skills, and it won't be legal." I looked at Detective Tanner to gauge his reaction to that. He didn't seem fazed, so I explained to Detective Tanner now, "Keith is a friend of Lewis's who has special computer skills. He's been hired by many law enforcement agencies in the past to hack sensitive information for them. We used him in the Craig Mazer case, and he came through big time. So, Tanner, do you have a list of the registered vehicles each detective drives?"

Tanner looked a little confused but said, "I do. But I'm going to pretend I didn't hear any part of this conversation. I will sort through some of the papers for you, and I think some information will be at the top of the pile. After I sort through it all, I'll head out. Call me after you work your end, OK?"

"Understood," I said.

With that, Detective Tanner stepped into the kitchen and started sorting through the boxes, making four different stacks.

Lewis said, "Keith said he's in, but I told him I'd call him back when you fill me in. So, what's the idea, Boss?"

"We need Keith to hack into the NYPD with the vehicles registered to each one of the dirty detectives and get their GPS locations. We'll then split up and follow them. We will stake them out until they get a job that gives them a duffel bag of cash. As soon as we see the drop, we follow the bag man. If we can see where he goes back to, maybe we can see where the cash comes from."

"This would've been easier if Tanner was still with them. It wouldn't take as long to know when they are getting a job. But I like the plan, and it's all we have at this point. I'll call Keith and tell him what the play is."

When I noticed Tanner slipping out to the elevator, I walked into the kitchen. At the top of each of the four stacks was the vehicle registration for each of the dirty detectives: Domingo, Chance, Waverly, and Grims.

CHAPTER 48

I HAD GOTTEN DETECTIVE Domingo and Detective Chance because they were riding together tonight. Lewis wanted to be on Detective Grims because he had a grudge to settle. Lewis also had a guy, Raul, on Detective Waverly. Waverly and Grims were still at the police station; Domingo and Chance were out riding around, but not headed anywhere specific that I could tell. I had done surveillance plenty of times before, but these were detectives and would be more vigilant than the perps I usually tail.

I had packed a thermos of coffee and a cooler of snacks and sandwiches. I wasn't sure how long I would be following them, but not long into their shift, their lights and sirens came on. I had to pick up speed and get closer than I'd like to be to keep up with them. I was hoping their attention would be focused on what's in front of them instead of what's behind.

I trailed them as they came up to a uniformed police officer in his police cruiser. The officer had someone pulled over. Why would detectives be sent to a routine traffic stop? I was parked just down the block and got out to get a better look. I couldn't hear what was being said, but within minutes, the uniformed officer got in his cruiser and pulled off. Then the man from the traffic stop popped his trunk and handed a bag to Detective Domingo and what seemed to be a folder or notebook, I couldn't be sure.

I called Lewis. "Hey, they just received a bag and some kind of folder. They didn't open the bag, so I'm not sure what's inside, but I'm going to follow the bagman anyway. I need you to pull off Grims and pick up the location of Domingo's car and see where they go."

"Got it, Boss. I have their location now and am heading that way. Angelo, don't approach that guy yet, just see where he goes. If we aren't sure what was in the bag, we can't blow our cover by pursuing them too soon."

"I got it, Lewis. Thank you."

I had gotten back to my car as Domingo and Chance pulled out. The other guy was just getting back into his car. I waited, but he just sat there. His car was running, but I couldn't see anything else. Maybe he was on his phone or looking up directions to where he was going next. Or maybe he was waiting for someone else?

Finally, he put on his turn signal and pulled out into traffic. I was able to catch up quickly, as traffic was moving slowly. While I was following him, Lewis texted that Domingo and Chance came back to the police station. Then a few minutes later, he said that they were on the move, and all four detectives were now in Domingo's car. He and his guy, Raul, were both following.

I had followed the bagman all the way downtown to a familiar place—city hall. He pulled into the parking garage. It was after business hours, but the garage was open twenty-four hours. I decided to try and park as close as possible without being seen. The man got out of his car, but I didn't recognize him. He walked out of the garage and into city hall. He swiped a badge, so I assumed he was an employee. Since city hall was closed, that's as far as I could go.

I went back to the parking garage and copied the license plate and VIN of the bagman's vehicle and snapped some pictures of the car. I got back into my car and called Lewis to see what they had.

"Lewis, where are you now?"

"We followed them to a storage facility. I'm sitting outside ready to pick them back up when they leave, but Raul went on foot into the storage facility. The facility is still open, so Raul is posing as someone who wants to purchase a storage unit. He got the guy to take him around the facility on a golf cart to look at units. I'm waiting for him to report back. What happened with your guy, the bagman?"

"Unfortunately, I don't recognize him, but he did enter city hall with a badge. Since it's closed, I couldn't follow him further. I got his plate and VIN, so hopefully Keith can get some more information on who he is."

Lewis said, "Well, that is interesting. Hey, hold on a second, Raul is coming up to my car now. I'm going to put you on speakerphone."

I heard Lewis say, "Raul, what did you find? I've got Angelo on the phone here."

Raul said, "I caught a glimpse of the detectives in their storage unit as they were closing the door. It looks like they have some kind of office set up in there, but I couldn't stop because I didn't want them to see me. The unit is number 26, and it's one of the thirty units they have on site that is temperature controlled and on the ground floor. I didn't see what was in the bag, but they had it with them."

I said, "Good work, guys. Let's pull out for tonight. We have some information to work with now. We can start piecing this together and follow them again if necessary. Lewis, I'll meet you back at your place."

"OK, Boss. I'll call Keith on my way back there."

CHAPTER 49

BY THE TIME LEWIS got back to his penthouse, Keith already had a name and address for the registration of the car. The car was an official city vehicle and was registered with city hall's address. Luckily, Keith wouldn't stop there and was able to get into the city hall records. The car was being leased out to the campaign manager of Mayor Daniels, a Carter Maxwell. Keith had also sent over pictures of Carter Maxwell, and I told Keith and Lewis that was the man I'd seen in the garage.

While Lewis got his research people on an extensive background of Mr. Maxwell, I did a quick online search for him. Carter Maxwell had been Mayor Daniels' campaign manager for the last eleven years, starting with his two terms as a senator and his current mayoral seat. He was known as "The Wonderkid" because of running successful campaigns since he was twenty-one years old. Strangely though, there was nothing about his life prior to twenty-one—no family listed or personal life before his career started.

"Hey, Lewis, get Keith back on the phone please," I said.

Once Lewis had Keith on speakerphone, I asked, "Hey, Keith, can you help us out with one more thing?"

Keith's gruff voice said, "Sure thing! I haven't had this much fun in a while. Whatcha got?"

"Do you think you could get into a storage lot's security system and disable all alarms and cameras?"

Keith said, "Yes, but I will need some information to do that. You'll need to get the specifications on the camera and alarm systems and an address. And I will need a login."

I said, "Great. In the morning, Lewis and I will go rent a storage unit. Hopefully their system is one that you can gain access to the cameras, but we'll figure it all out somehow."

▪ ▪ ▪

The next morning, Lewis, Raul, and I drove to Prime Storage in Bronx, New York. Raul and I went in, and we asked to see the biggest units available. It was a 10x15 storage unit on the ground floor of the building, in a large open space, with a garage door opening to the back of the facility. This must have been where the guy drove Raul the night before.

As we were walking around the thirty units on the ground floor, the clerk said, "We have four units available. Numbers 2, 10, 27, and 30. Would you like to see one opened?"

"Yes," I said. "Could we please see unit 27? We like the placement of that one."

He opened the door of the unit. Just your typical concrete floors and metal walls. We didn't really care what it looked like, just what it could provide us. He told us about the temperature control of the building and the cameras and security that would protect our unit and all the other units. He said that they have an insurance policy for an extra $10 a month that would insure up to $50,000 of items.

As he finished with his spiel, I got a text message. I looked up from my phone and told the clerk, "We'll take it. But can we get a copy of the cameras and alarm systems specifications? We like to be extremely careful with our equipment."

He said, "That will all come in your information packet when we finalize your contract. Let's go back up front and get your paperwork done. Then I'll give you a login and a temporary password for the access to your live camera in the area outside your locker. How long did you want to rent for? We have month-to-month, biannual, and yearly pricing."

I filled out all the paperwork and got myself a storage unit, at least for a month. He handed me the packet, which had all the information I needed. Then he set up my login and gave me a temporary password. He shook our hands and handed us the keys.

We went out to Lewis's car. When we got in, I said, "Did you get it?"

Lewis said, "Of course, Boss."

CHAPTER 50

WE CALLED KEITH ON the way back to Lewis's place. We gave him pictures of all the packet materials, my login information, Lewis's pictures, and the administrator's login information. See, the nice thing about the twenty-four-hour storage facilities is that there is usually only one worker on duty at a time. While the clerk was showing us around, Lewis took pictures of the entire security system and found a Post-it note with all the logins and alarm codes. Keith said he would get back to us when he was able to get things set up.

We decided to take a detour and headed to city hall. We still hadn't been able to find anything out about Carter Maxwell's life before age twenty-one. It's like he didn't exist before then. We thought that maybe Lewis could ask Mayor Daniels to arrange a meeting with Mr. Maxwell, posing as a contributor to the mayoral campaign. Obviously, Mayor Daniels already knows us, but…money talks.

At city hall, we made it to Graham's desk, but he wouldn't let us go any further. He said that the mayor was out of the office all day. Then Lewis said, "I'm looking to support Mayor Daniels for reelection. Is there someone I can talk to instead then?"

Graham just shook his head and said, "I'm sorry, guys, but Mayor Daniels told me to not allow any of you back into his office."

I offered, "You know that Mr. Pollard is part of the De Beers diamond family, right, Graham?"

Lewis tossed out, "I guess I'll have to put my half a million dollars into someone else's campaign. We'll see you around, Graham."

Graham stood up suddenly as we were walking away and said, "Hey, wait! I will schedule an appointment with Mr. Carter Maxwell, the mayor's campaign manager. Mayor Daniels didn't say you couldn't meet with others on his staff, just not him. So, I see no problem with that. Mr. Maxwell will be available two days from now. Will that work?"

"Yes," Lewis said, "that would be great. Thank you for your help, Graham. We'll see you in two days."

As we were walking out of city hall, I told Lewis, "I hope you have a plan. We have two days to get more facts about Carter Maxwell. If he's connected with all of this like I think he is, he will know who you and I are. We could be walking into a trap."

"I do, Boss. You're right, we do need more information. But we have Keith now, and we can be the ones setting the trap. Keith texted we are good to go tonight. So, for now, we need to focus on the storage center. Let me handle Carter Maxwell."

"You're right, Lewis. We need to find out what Carter Maxwell gave the dirty detectives and go from there."

CHAPTER 51

IT WAS MIDNIGHT AND the storage center was empty except for the night clerk. I said hello, swiped my card, and strolled back to my unit. I was carrying a small tool bag. I unlocked the unit I rented, stepped inside, and closed the door. I sent the text.

The alarm systems started beeping for thirty seconds straight and then silence. I pulled open the storage unit door, checked the cameras, and saw all the red lights were off. Kieth had disabled everything. I called Lewis.

"Hey, do you have a location for all the detectives?"

Lewis said, "All clear, Boss. The GPS has them all at the police station, and Raul said that none of them have left since 11 p.m. Do you want me to come in now?"

"Yeah, head in. I'll start on the lock."

By the time Lewis came in the door, I had finished picking the key lock on the detectives' unit. Lewis rolled up the unit door. Once he had the door up, he said, "Keith said we have nine minutes before the system backup turns the alarms and cameras back on; that was three minutes ago."

"Got it," I said. "We better get started. I'll take the bag."

Lewis said he would take the cabinets. There were white metal cabinets lining one wall of the storage unit. The rest of the space was taken up by a table and four chairs. The bag that I had seen Carter Maxwell deliver the other day was sitting in the middle of the table.

I unzipped the bag and was about to look inside when Lewis exclaimed, "What the…"

I turned around to discover Lewis had half the cabinets opened, and they were all filled with cash. Some of it was in tight bundles, while others were just piles of loose cash. There had to be over two million dollars.

I said, "Yeah, that is crazy. Keep opening and take pictures, but don't touch anything. I need to see what's in this bag."

I turned back to the bag, peered inside, and found all the same files that were in piles in Lewis's penthouse. These were the original documents that Detective Tanner said were taken by the mayor's office. I opened the bag as best I could and started taking pictures without moving anything inside the bag. I carefully zipped the bag back up and helped Lewis finish inspecting the cabinets.

There wasn't much else besides a few empty duffel bags in the rest of the cabinets. No papers or any kind of documents that would help us know for sure where all this money came from.

We took as many pictures as possible, closed all the cabinets, and wiped everything down. We closed the unit door and put the lock back on. I closed my unit, and we headed out the back exit. Two minutes still left to spare.

CHAPTER 52

WE KNEW THE DOCUMENTS came from Carter Maxwell and that the mayor's office is the one who ordered the police to turn over all documents. But we still couldn't be sure where all the money was coming from. So, while we waited for our meeting with Carter Maxwell, we were back on our stakeout of the dirty detectives.

I also hadn't heard from Vanesa since the day at the mayor's office. I tried her cell. No answer. I called Lewis, and he said that his guys stated that she hadn't left since that day either. Maybe she was still mad at me.

Lewis texted that Grims was on the move and he was following. I texted back a thumbs-up and to let us know if we need to head to his location to pick up a bagman. Right after that, I saw Domingo's car roll away. I picked up his tail and texted Raul and Lewis. They both replied OK.

I tailed Domingo for a few miles. It was just after midnight when he pulled into an alley. I needed to park the car so I could try to get in better position to see what was going on in the alley. But there weren't any parking spots anywhere. Finally, I decided to park in a tow zone and hope for the best.

I looked down at my phone. Lewis had texted: *False alarm with Grims, just getting food.*

I wrote back: *Make sure he goes back to police station and then come to Domingo's location. I'm on foot following into an alley. No visual yet.*

He said he would be there soon, and Raul said he would stay on the three at the police station. I peeked around the corner down the alley. I couldn't see anyone, but Domingo's car was still running. I didn't see him inside the vehicle either. I decided to go down the alley to see who he was meeting with, but I stopped dead in my tracks when I heard Domingo yelling.

He said, "I thought you were taking care of the rich guy and that PI! You said you had it handled! Do I need to step in and make sure they don't interfere anymore? And how did you not know that Detective Tanner was a plant for Internal Affairs?"

Someone responded, but they were not nearly as loud as Domingo. I couldn't see or hear who Domingo was talking to. I couldn't see either of them from where I was.

Domingo started yelling again, "You better handle it, or I will!"

I heard him approaching quickly in my direction. I jumped into the dumpster I was hiding behind. I closed the lid quickly but made sure it didn't slam. I heard his car peel out of the alley, and I waited five minutes so that I wasn't seen. I texted Lewis: *Pick up Domingo's location and follow. I had to trash the surveillance to avoid being spotted.*

He replied: *Got it, Boss. I'm two minutes behind him. It looks like he's heading toward police, but I'll make sure.*

■ ■ ■

Domingo was back at the police station with the other three. I pulled up behind Lewis's car and got in his passenger seat. Immediately he asked, "What's that smell?"

I told him what happened and that I couldn't see who Domingo was talking to, but that they definitely knew who we were. He laughed at me and told me to go back to his place and shower. He also said he'd send me the cleaning bill for the car.

I said, "Thanks. I'll head back, but you and Raul need to be careful. If they know who we are and are concerned about us, they may shoot on sight. So, don't be seen."

Nothing happened the rest of the night. The detectives stayed at the police station the entire night. I wondered if they were lying low with the investigation almost putting them away. It was thrown out, but they may have decided to stay away from their nefarious activities for a while…which wouldn't really work for us.

CHAPTER 53

WE ALL CAUGHT A couple of hours of sleep, but we were back up by ten in the morning. I tried Vanesa again. Still no answer. I asked Lewis to try. No answer.

"Are you sure she's still at the safe house?" I asked Lewis.

"My guys said she hasn't left. There are two guys outside the house and one staying inside. Let me call Greg, who's my inside guy, and double-check. Maybe I'll have him ask her to call us back."

Lewis called, but it just rang and went to voice mail. He called his guys outside, and they answered. They said she hadn't left. He asked them to go check out the house and see why Greg wasn't answering.

Two minutes later, Lewis got a phone call back. He said, "We need to go. Greg has been killed, and Vanesa is gone!"

Within fifteen minutes, we were at the safe house we had put Vanesa up in. We called Detective Tanner, and he met us there. We knew we had to call this into the police, but we wanted to check out the scene first. Tanner told us to look but not to touch anything.

We gave the living room a once-over. There had been a small struggle. Only the coffee table had been knocked over, but it may have just been from Greg falling onto it. Someone had surprised him. He had no marks on his hands or arms from fighting someone off. He had been strangled by the attacker.

We moved on to Vanesa's room. Her computer was gone, but her phone was still on the bedside table. There were five missed calls on the phone, but I didn't try to unlock it. She must have been taken the night before, so they had at least a twelve-hour head start on us. We made the call to the police to report the murder. Tanner told us he couldn't be there and that he would meet up with us later.

The police questioning was exhaustive, but we told them what they needed to know. What they needed to know was that Vanesa was working on a big class action lawsuit and was in a safe house being watched by bodyguards due to threats to her life. We had told them that the threats were not reported to the police but that we were being cautious with the protection of Vanesa.

We had just lost another four hours looking for Vanesa, but we also had lost a member of Lewis's team. He deserved our respect as well, and Lewis would take care of his family and funeral arrangements. Lewis and I drove to the now widow's house and broke the news. She was devastated but knew the risks of his job and was always worried that this day would come. We stayed with Greg's wife until her mother was able to come and be with her grieving daughter.

Finally, we headed back into the city. We were exhausted, emotionally drained, and realized we hadn't eaten anything all day. We knew we had a long night ahead of us, so we headed to Mancino's for a quick bite so we could trudge on.

CHAPTER 54

LEWIS AND I EACH had a slice of pizza as we called Keith again. We had him put out a trace locator for Vanesa's computer, but he said that it wasn't turned on. He said that he would set up an alert and would let us know the second the computer came on. We also called Lewis's team that was stationed with Camila Jefferson's family. Since the bad guys had somehow found Vanesa's safe house, then we needed to move Camila and her family again.

As we left Mancino's, Lewis and I each grabbed a slice to go. Detective Tanner called with the coroner's report. It was as expected: Greg was killed by strangulation between six and eight the night before. He also said that the forensics team was still at the safe house looking for evidence, but as of now, the only prints they had found were Greg's and Vanesa's.

After Tanner hung up, I said to Lewis, "Why didn't they clean this up with the dirty detectives? They don't usually leave bodies behind. They make them disappear. And if they had been called in, we would've been there."

"I know, Boss, I was thinking the same thing. But maybe they made a mistake. Or maybe I called my guys, and they were able to get there before the detectives were able to? Or maybe they wanted us to find the body?"

"I'm not sure either, Lewis, but I think I know where we need to start looking. You have your meeting with Carter Maxwell tomorrow morning, right?"

"Yeah. What are you thinking?"

"When you go in, play nice. But after he feels comfortable and that you're going to give him money for the campaign, turn on him. Press him on the detectives and the money he is receiving from Fibayson. He may not answer, and he may kick you out, but you're great at reading people. Once you press him, see if he gets defensive or clams up completely. See if he starts slipping at all. I know you can do this, Lewis."

"Sounds good," Lewis said. "Now, what are we going to do about finding Vanesa?"

"I don't know, and that upsets me a lot. I'm hoping that if they do have her, they will reach out and give us something. Or hopefully they turn on the computer. I guess for tonight, we focus on moving Camila and—"

"Sorry to cut you off, Boss, but that's my team calling from Camila's safe house. Let me take this."

Lewis got on the phone, and within a minute, he yelled, "What do you mean gone?!? Where is Mason? He's been killed too? We're on our way!"

CHAPTER 55

WE RUSHED TO THE safe house. On the way over, Lewis explained to me that Camila and her family were gone, and that the man guarding the back of the house, Mason, was dead. He also told me that it had to have happened within the last two hours because his guys had been doing two-hour check-ins with each other, and they were all accounted for in the last check-in. When Mason didn't check in at the next one, they investigated and found him dead, and Camila and her family were gone.

I went into the home while Lewis was out in front going ballistic on his men. I had never seen or heard Lewis like that before, but over the last twenty-four hours, he had lost two men, and it was taking a toll on him. I needed to assess the situation and let Lewis do his thing.

When I walked through the house, it was a weird scene. I guess I had expected it to be a mess and things broken. But everything was in its place and undisturbed. As I walked through the bedrooms, all their clothing was gone, as were their personal items. It's like they had packed up and left. So, if they had let them bring their belongings, there was hope that they were still alive.

When I came back outside, I could still hear Lewis, but he seemed to have calmed down some. I stepped up to the group, and Lewis said, "Find anything, Angelo?"

"It looks like they went willingly with whoever took them. There doesn't seem to have been a struggle, and all their personal belongings are gone. I believe they are all unharmed for now, but we need to find them before they get hurt."

"OK, Boss." Lewis turned to his men and instructed, "Please call this into the police and notify Mason's family personally. I can't handle another notification today. Also, call me immediately if any of the cops that show up are named Domingo, Grims, Chance, or Waverly."

They both nodded their heads solemnly and started making phone calls. Lewis and I walked through the house one more time so that he could get his eyes on it. Then he went back out so he could say his goodbye to Mason. We headed out shortly so that we wouldn't be there when the police arrived.

Placing a hand on Lewis's shoulder, I said, "Hey, man, you're going to be OK. We're going to catch these guys. I promise."

Lewis said, "I know we are, but I'm not used to losing people. My guys are the best. It's like they know exactly what we are doing and how we are doing it. I don't like it."

We decided the best plan was to try and track any of Camila's family's phones. We didn't do an exhaustive search of the house, but we didn't see any phones anywhere. We had left the safe house approximately thirty minutes ago, and we were almost back in the city when Lewis got a phone call. He put it on speaker.

"Hey, Mr. Pollard, you said to call if one of those detectives showed up. There's a Detective Chance and a Detective Waverly here, and they came up with some wild thoughts on what went on here."

"What did they say?" Lewis asked. "Were you with them the whole time they searched?"

"Well, no, they wouldn't let us. It's like they knew what they were looking for already. They came back to us and questioned us for a few minutes, but not much really. Then they said that they were ruling Mason a suicide and that the family left of their own accord."

Lewis and I both yelled, "WHAT?!??"

"He said that they found a gun near Mason's body and that it was a self-inflicted wound. But I never saw a gun. Did you, Mr. Pollard?"

Lewis shook his head and said, "No, but that doesn't mean they didn't put one there. Why do they think Camila's family left on their own?"

"Well, he said they found a note that was written to Miss Galloway. They told me it said: *Sorry, but they offered me five million dollars to walk away. I must do what's best for my family. – Camila.*"

Defiant, I said, "Where did they find this note? I didn't see any note!"

"Sorry, he didn't say. But like I said before, they came in and had their conclusions very quickly."

Lewis asked, "Can you ask them what they are even doing there? This is not within the city limits. This should be a county case."

"Sorry, Boss. They left already. They said the case was closed."

CHAPTER 56

I **AWOKE THE NEXT** day in the Roxy Hotel New York. We couldn't be sure what was going on, so we had rooms for me, Joe, Detective Tanner, and Lewis. Nothing was going the way we had planned. The case against the dirty detectives had been all but wrapped up, Vanesa had been finishing up her class action lawsuit with Camila's testimony, but now it was all chaos.

I had spent half the night looking through video surveillance of the storage facility, but the detectives had not been there since the case against them came out. Keith still couldn't track Vanesa's computer, and all of Camila's family's phones were all transmitting signals from the safe house. Probably courtesy of Detectives Chance and Waverly planting them back at the house.

Lewis still had his meeting with Carter Maxwell this morning, so I gathered everyone in my room to go over the plan for this meeting. I had also invited Agent Grady Humble in for the meeting. At that point, the FBI had nothing on the bombing of the field office, so he was anxious for any help.

Joe was going to attend the meeting as Lewis's money manager, Joseph Angelo. Safety in numbers. Detective Tanner and I would sit on Carter Maxwell's car and follow him if he left right after the meeting. We would also be listening in on the meeting through Joe's phone being left on for us. We couldn't risk any other type of recording devices in case Carter was onto us. Agent Humble would also be in on the call, recording it from the hotel.

Detective Tanner and I went an hour before the meeting to stake out the garage. We found Carter Maxwell's car, which was a good indication that he was in and would keep the appointment with Lewis. Joe and Lewis left Grady in the hotel, and Joe started the phone call with both Grady and me on the line. Joe checked that we were both on, and after we replied we were good, we muted our sides of the line.

We all waited as we heard the echo of Joe and Lewis's footsteps through the tiled halls of the building. They stopped when they'd probably made it to the desk of the mayor's assistant, Graham.

Lewis said, "We are here for our meeting with Mr. Maxwell."

Graham replied, "I'll let him know you are here, Mr. Pollard. And who is this joining you?"

"This is my money manager, Joseph Angelo."

"OK, please have a seat, and I'll let you know when he is ready for you," Graham said.

After about five minutes, we heard Graham say, *"Mr. Maxwell will see you both now. His office is just past Mayor Daniels', on the right."*

Detective Tanner and I heard the door open to Carter Maxwell's office. *Carter said, "Mr. Pollard, I heard that you wanted to donate money to Mayor Daniels' campaign for reelection. How can I help you make the right decision today? And hello, Joe Barsotti, so nice to meet you."*

Well, he'd made Joe. So, he knew who they were, but how would he play it?

"Um…, hi, Mr. Maxwell," Joe stammered out.

Lewis said, "OK, so you know who we are, and you know that I have no willingness to donate to Mayor Daniels' campaign. Why did you still agree to meet with us?"

Carter laughed a little. He said, "Because, Mr. Pollard, while you all are here, I'm sure Angelo isn't far away. And there are other things in movement. We know that you were tracking the detectives' vehicles, and we didn't need any tails today. We have precious cargo being moved, and we didn't need you there. Also, don't bother trying to track them anymore. All vehicles have been swapped out. We just couldn't risk you being near them and interfering.

"So, I kept the meeting because I wanted you here. Thank you for agreeing to this. Oh, and Angelo, Vanesa sends her regards as well."

I called Lewis's phone. "Just get out of there! We will pick him up when he leaves!"

CHAPTER 57

I CALLED AGENT HUMBLE. "Did you get all of that?"

"Yeah, but it's not enough for us to move on a government official."

Starting to get angry, I said, "What do you mean not enough? He said he had Vanesa! He basically admitted to working with the dirty detectives!"

Grady calmly said, "I know, Angelo, but he didn't admit to any wrongdoing. He said that Vanesa sends her regards, but we don't know for sure that he has her. Also, he actually implicated you and Lewis for tracking police officials' vehicles. So, at the end of the day, the tape I have can never see the light of day. We will need to catch him working with the detectives doing something illegal or holding Vanesa against her will. I'm sorry, Angelo, but I can only work within the limits of the law."

Frustrated, I just hung up the phone. I wasn't mad at Grady. I understood his point of view, but I couldn't just let this go. Lewis texted that he and Joe were heading back to the hotel and that he needed a minute to clear his head. Tanner and I were going to stay right here and wait for Carter Maxwell to come out to his car.

▪ ▪ ▪

We waited hours, but he never came out. Eventually we concluded that he must have swapped cars as well. We called Keith. Keith had figured out quickly that Carter Maxwell had rented a car but said that it would take some time to hack into the GPS of the vehicle.

Lewis and Joe had been looking over the arson cases again while we were waiting for Carter to come out. So, we went and met up with them to see if they had figured anything new out.

When Tanner and I reached the hotel room, Joe was pacing the room waving a piece of paper around. I said, "What's going on, Joe?"

Joe wondered, "Why didn't I make the connection before?"

Tanner asked, "What connection is that?"

Joe went on, "I always wondered what they were achieving by burning the old records. I know that medical facilities and places like it have to keep records for a number of years, but at this point, all things should be digital. Anything that Lucy or Camila would have found would be saved in a digital database. There must have been something else that they were trying to destroy."

I asked, "Do you have any idea what that may be?"

Joe headed toward the door as he replied, "I need to confirm my theory before I discuss it. It may be nothing, but I need to go see one of the guys who responded to the second fire. I was at the first, and there might have been something. I'll be back."

CHAPTER 58

I **RAN OUT TO** catch up with Joe. I told him it wasn't safe for him to go alone and that I was coming with him. Lewis had a car come and pick us up. On the ride, I said, "Where are we going, Joe?"

Joe said, "Look, I remembered noticing a second damaged area. It wasn't affected by the fire, but there was accelerant all over the place. I think the ethanol was used to destroy test samples. There were exploded tubes all over the place and were considered to be broken by the heat of the fire. I wasn't thinking about it at the time, but the heat of the fire would not have reached that room before we put out the fire. I need to talk to one of the firefighters on the second fire or Captain Lamke and see if one of them saw the same situation."

"Why would they do that?" I asked.

"Ethanol can be used to break down molecular compounds. I think that those test tubes were the ones showing what problems there could be with their drug, so they wanted the evidence destroyed."

"Why wouldn't they start the fire in those rooms then?"

"My only guess is that they wanted to make sure that the compounds were wiped clean by the ethanol and expected the fire to come through there eventually. But if the fire didn't make it there, then those vials would have already been destroyed."

I said, "I'm not sure why they still wouldn't start the fire in there, but I'm following your line of thinking. Let's see what Captain Lamke has to say. We're here."

We entered the firehouse, and luckily everyone was there. We went straight to Captain Lamke's office. Joe asked him about the second fire and about the ethanol. Captain Lamke thought about it for a while before answering. Eventually he said, "From what I can remember is that there was accelerant throughout the building, but the only fire was in the records room."

Joe then said, "OK, think if there was a room with test tubes or vials. Was there broken glass all over the place?"

Captain Lamke thought for a bit again and then said, "I don't recall, but we videoed that whole scene because it was similar to the first fire, and arson was suspected, so we documented the whole walk-through. Let me go check for the video log."

He took us into Nathan Grimble's office. He said, "This is going to take me a few minutes. Sorry, but since Nathan has gone missing, we've been a little unorganized. I sure wish he would come back soon. I've been worried about him."

Joe gave me a look, but I just shook my head. We couldn't involve anyone else in this mess. Too many people had been hurt already, and hopefully Joe would continue to understand the need for silence.

Captain Lamke said, "Here it is. Since the case was closed by the police and ruled accidental, it's no longer an open case, so you guys can just take it if you want."

I said, "Thank you, Captain Lamke. We will. And thank you for all you do for our city."

"I appreciate that, Angelo. Your brother is a real asset here, and I hope he gets back to work soon," he said as he shot Joe a look.

With the flash drive in hand, we started to head out as Joe said, "I hear you, Cap, and I'll be back as soon as possible."

▪ ▪ ▪

We took the flash drive back to the hotel, and Joe explained to everyone his theory as he rewatched the walk-through. The same thing he had seen at the first fire tracked with the second fire. They had destroyed all the test tubes and vials in each location prior to the fires being started.

Joe said, "I'm not sure what it helps, but at least now we know the true target, and the fire was probably just a distraction."

Lewis said, "Nice work, Joe. Maybe Angelo should hire you as part of our team?"

Joe laughed and said, "I'm not sure I'm cut out for that line of work, and I love being a firefighter. But I also love my son, and I need to go back and check on him and my ex-wife. I'll catch up with you guys in a few hours."

Joe left and wouldn't allow anyone to come with him this time. He said he knew it was dangerous, but this was his family, and he needed to make sure they were OK.

CHAPTER 59

LEWIS, DETECTIVE TANNER, AND I were still sitting in the hotel room trying to figure out our next move and waiting for Keith to track Carter Maxwell's car when my phone rang. It was Joe on his burner phone. I answered, "Hey, Joe, that wasn't very long." But it wasn't Joe on the other end.

The distorted voice said, "We have your brother. We don't want any more blood on our hands, but we will do what is necessary if you don't comply."

"What is it that you want?" I asked as calmly as possible.

"We need all the files you have on the detectives. We need all the surveillance video and equipment from the storage units. And we want Internal Affairs Detective Tanner."

"Where is Vanesa? Is she still alive?"

"We are in control here, Mr. Barsotti. Vanesa is still alive. Maybe I'll let her wave goodbye to you when you bring what I've asked for. You have twenty-four hours."

The line went dead. No instructions of where to meet or whether I agreed to their terms. I turned to Tanner and Lewis. "Did you get all that?"

Lewis said, "Yeah, Boss. I hit the recorder as soon as you signaled. Good thing Grady left this here. What should we do now?"

Detective Tanner said, "We can't just give them what they want. I have no problem being the sacrificial lamb. I've lived a good life. But we cannot give them all that they're asking for."

"Of course not, Tanner," I said. "But we have twenty-four hours to figure out the plan for the swap. Also, from the way the caller was talking, I believe that was our friend Carter Maxwell on the line. Lewis, call Keith and tell him we need that trace of Carter Maxwell's rental immediately."

▪ ▪ ▪

Keith called back within an hour. His gruff voice came over the speakerphone, "OK, guys, I found the car. I had to take some not-so-legal shortcuts. Sorry, Detective Tanner. But he's at city hall. Are you sure he was the caller?"

"I can't be a hundred percent sure because of the voice distortion, but how he spoke felt exactly how I heard him earlier today with Lewis." I asked Keith, "Can you track the vehicle's path for the day? Maybe he just got back there?"

Detective Tanner said, "He may have just been the caller. I doubt he or Mayor Daniels get their hands personally dirty—that's what they have the detectives for."

Keith said, "He's right. It's probably the detectives who have your brother and Vanesa. And I can't find them in the logs for any cars from the department. And all their personal vehicles are not registered. I'm sorry I couldn't be more help. But Carter Maxwell is driving a silver 2022 Hyundai Santa Fe with Texas license plates. Call me if I can do anything else. I'll keep trying to ping Vanesa's computer in the meantime. Talk soon."

We all voiced our appreciation and said goodbye. I said, "Lewis, can you get a guy over to city hall to follow Carter Maxwell's car if he leaves?"

Lewis was about to talk when Detective Tanner cut him off, "I'll go. It may not be a safe tail, and Lewis, you have suffered enough loss on this already. Can you get me a car though?"

"Sure thing, Tanner," Lewis said. "Be careful and stay in constant contact."

CHAPTER 60

IT HAD BEEN SIX hours since the phone call—eighteen hours to figure out what to do. We had already moved Joe's son and ex-wife into Lewis's penthouse. We had been in touch with Agent Humble, and he had assembled a small tactical team for the rescue of Joe. There had been no movement of Carter Maxwell's rental car.

We had also set up a geolocation map with Keith. He was our eye in the sky, making sure he was still watching over each of us. He also had tried to trace Joe's burner phone but said that it must have been destroyed right after the call because it was no longer transmitting.

■　■　■

It had been twelve hours when we received the next call. The distorted voice said, "So, do you agree to our terms? Or do we need to make sure you never see your brother again?"

I said, "We agree, and we have everything you're asking for. Where will we meet?"

"There's an abandoned warehouse on the north side of the Brooklyn Bridge. I'll send the location. You, Lewis, and

Tanner. I do not want to see Agent Humble or any of his FBI buddies there. Understand?"

"Got it. When?"

"One hour."

The line went dead. I received a text with the location. And then my phone began ringing. It was Detective Tanner. I answered, "I was just about to call you. We have a location."

Tanner said, "Carter Maxwell is on the move. Should I go with you or stay on him?"

"He may be heading to the same place, but just come pick us up. We will deal with him later. I need to get Joe."

"On my way."

I texted Agent Humble the location and the time. I wasn't about to go into a trap without backup, regardless of what the voice had said. I just hoped it was the right call.

Detective Tanner picked us up. We had a stack of blank papers in a folder, but nothing that they had asked for. We needed them to think we were playing ball. The location was twenty minutes away. We would be early.

CHAPTER 61

WE ARRIVED FIFTEEN MINUTES before the scheduled time. We didn't see any other cars in the area. We walked around the perimeter of the building. All the windows and doors were boarded up, except for one door that was slightly ajar. We didn't go in right away.

I texted Grady, and he replied that he would be in the area right at the meet time and that we shouldn't go in before he was set up. He wouldn't come in with us or even be right on the building, but he would be within reach. I trusted that would be the case.

When the appointed time came, we still hadn't seen anyone arrive. I didn't like it. Something was off. But we entered through the only accessible door and walked into an open, dilapidated building. There was fallen debris from rotting building materials everywhere. The only thing placed with intention was a table in in the middle of the room. A lone phone sat on a table. It began ringing.

We slowly turned toward one another, cautious and wondering if we should answer it. It could be a bomb, which could easily take us all out. But it could be Joe or Vanesa. So, I walked over and picked up the phone.

I wasn't ready for what I heard. "Hello, Angelo. I'm sorry for what I've put you through, but you just couldn't let it go. I thought the death of your wife, the deaths of others, the bombs, and the control we had over the police would get you to go away. But you just kept coming."

I was speechless. I couldn't even form a word, much less a sentence. My head was spinning, immediately going through all the things I might have missed.

The caller continued, "I knew you wouldn't come here without Grady, and I couldn't risk being caught yet. I have a job to do, and my family comes first.

"As for Joe, if you want to see him alive again, you will walk away from this. The people I work for have wanted you and Lewis dead for a long time now, and I can only hold them off if you stop. Maybe someday I can explain, and you'll listen, but now is not the time. Goodbye."

The line went dead, and I fell to my knees. I threw the phone across the warehouse. Tanner and Lewis rushed over. Lewis asked, "What did they say? Is Joe OK?"

Tanner asked, "Are they coming?"

I started to speak a couple of times, but nothing came out. Eventually, I was able to mutter, "Vanesa…"

Lewis yelled, "Did they kill her? What is going on, Angelo? Talk to us!"

I snapped out of it enough to say, "No, she's not dead. She was the caller."

CHAPTER 62

TANNER AND LEWIS FINALLY got me in the car, and we went to meet up with Grady. I was able to recount for them the entire conversation—well, the one-sided conversation from Vanesa. They had many questions, as did I, but I needed to focus on how to get Joe back safely.

Lewis asked, "Where does that leave us, Boss? What should we do?"

"We need to drop Lucy's case…" I paused, "for now. And not completely. We need to go back over the last year, since Vanesa entered our lives. We need to think over how much she knows from us, and if there's anything we know that she doesn't. And we need Keith to do a DEEP dive on Vanesa now!"

While Lewis called Keith to fill him in, I was lost in my thoughts. Did Vanesa kill my wife or have her killed? Is Camila still alive? How could I have missed this? Was my attraction to Vanesa blinding me? Was I so focused on the goal of finding justice for Lucy and the emotions her death cause that it clouded my judgment?

I snapped out of it quickly. I decided to push all those thoughts away and focus on the task at hand. I needed to get

Joe back and put an end to all of this. Lewis tapped me on the shoulder.

He said, "Keith found some preliminary things about Vanesa…a link to Carter Maxwell. He changed his last name three years ago. His real last name is Galloway…Carter Galloway!"

"What?! They're related?" I yelled.

"Yes," Lewis said, "he's her brother!"

Again, I was hit in the face with my complete lack of knowing the facts. Usually, we know the people we are working with, but we made assumptions about Vanesa. She came to us through a mutual working relationship on the Mazer case, and we never questioned any of it. Then she dropped us information about Lucy, and she had me hook, line, and sinker. We followed blindly, but her real intention was to always be a step ahead of us. And if I was being truthful, she was more than a few steps ahead. And now she had Joe.

"Lewis, see what else Keith can find on Vanesa," I said, "but tell him first we need to know Carter Maxwell's location!"

Lewis was still on the phone with Keith, who overheard the request and was able to locate Carter Maxwell's rental car. It was still at city hall. I said, "I guess we'll have to wait until morning, because there's no way to get into city hall after hours without access."

Grady stepped in and said, "I think I can help with that. This is a kidnapping case, which makes it federal. And if Carter Maxwell is working with the detectives, from what you have told me, they are responsible for the bombing at the field office, which is my case. So, I can use my status as an FBI agent to get us through security."

I said, "Great! What are we standing around here for then?"

CHAPTER 63

WHEN WE ARRIVED AT city hall, we parked in the garage right next to Carter Maxwell's rental. Detective Tanner volunteered to stay in the car in case Maxwell came out before we got to him.

As soon as we entered the front doors, security stopped us. It took less than thirty seconds for Agent Humble to get us beyond security and in the elevator going up to the mayor's floor.

The place was empty and dark. Only a few safety lights were on. But light shone from under Carter Maxwell's office door. We headed straight for it. I stormed in and yelled, "Where is my brother?"

Unfortunately, I wasn't going to get an answer. Carter Maxwell was at his desk, but he was dead. Lewis and Grady were right behind me, and both looked on in shock. It looked like a suicide, but it all felt very staged. It looked like someone had killed him and then set the scene. Grady and Lewis agreed.

We stepped out of the office, so we didn't disturb anything. Grady called it into the police while I called Detective Tanner. I told him that Grady was on the phone with the police and that his dirty cop friends would probably be showing up. He said to call when we were ready to leave. Since the cameras and security would have seen the three of us, we decided to wait for the police to come.

▪ ▪ ▪

It didn't take long for the detectives to arrive. And not one, but all four of the dirty detectives were there. Domingo was the definitive leader, and he went straight into the office. Chance, Waverly, and Grims split us up and questioned each of us why we were there. I had the pleasure of meeting Detective Chance. He went through the routine questions but didn't care to really listen to my answers. He was just acting like he was doing his job in front of the patrol officers that were there. When he finished, he said, "Thanks for your time. Make sure you stay in town in case we need to talk to you again, Mr. Barsotti." But then leaned in close and whispered so only I could hear, "You better run. We warned you."

He walked back to Maxwell's office and went in with Domingo. Grims and Waverly also finished their pseudo inter- rogations and joined them. I went over to Grady and Lewis and asked, "Did either of you get a warning?"

Lewis said, "Yeah, Grims told me I'd be inside the car the next time they bomb it if we didn't get away from this immediately."

Grady said, "No, but I guess they knew I was FBI and wouldn't threaten an agent. Let's get out of here."

As I passed the office door, I saw Domingo on the phone, and the only thing I heard was "I warned you."

CHAPTER 64

DETECTIVE TANNER WAS WAITING for us in the city hall parking garage. We all got in the car and headed back to the hotel. I said, "Domingo and the detectives murdered Carter Maxwell."

"Why do you say that?" Lewis asked. "I thought they were all working with him."

"I'm not sure on the why yet, but I heard Domingo say 'I warned you' to someone on the phone. And when I was following him the other night, he had met up with someone in the alley. I could only hear Domingo's side of the conversation because he was so mad that the other person wasn't handling Lewis and me like they said they could. So, either the other person was Carter Maxwell or Vanesa. And I'm guessing it was Vanesa, and that's why Carter is dead."

Grady got in the conversation by asking, "Why would they kill Carter Maxwell? Why not kill Vanesa if he had warned her? Don't they need Carter to control the mayor?"

"OK, let's say he met with Carter," I said. "Then why would he call Vanesa and say, 'I warned you'? She must have been the person he met with in the alley. And remember when we came to the mayor's office and Vanesa was already here? She must have the mayor's ear, or the mayor is completely involved himself and working with her."

Lewis said, "Let me play devil's advocate here. How do you know he called Vanesa? It could have been anyone on the phone, like the mayor."

"You're right, Lewis. I don't know for sure, but I know it in my bones."

"OK, Boss," Lewis said. "But like you always say, we need to find the facts."

"I know, I know. But I must follow my gut on this one. For Joe. For Lucy. The fact is, we know Vanesa has Joe and the detectives killed Carter. Grady, is there anything you can do to get these detectives off the streets?"

Detective Tanner spoke up for the first time, "I had a whole case put against them, and the mayor's office threw it out and confiscated all my files. But Angelo has a copy of all of it."

Grady looked distraught. Finally, he said, "I cannot get involved unless they crossed state lines or did something directly to the government. If you can prove that they bombed our offices, then I can go after them. So, how do we do that?"

"Hank Dupont is dead, and he was our only certain link to them and the bombings. But if we could somehow get one of the detectives to turn on the others…" I turned to Tanner. "Any ideas on which would flip?"

"If I had to guess," Tanner said, "it would probably be Waverly. He is the lowest ranked on the team and they let him know it. He gets the lowest cut of the money but shares all the risks."

"OK, let's start there. Lewis, you and Tanner get with Keith and find out everything there is to know on Detective Waverly. Grady, you and I need to find Joe."

CHAPTER 65

GRADY AND I DROPPED Lewis and Tanner off at the hotel to work, and we went to Lewis's. We went upstairs to the penthouse and grabbed the files for Grady to look through while we drove around. Lewis had called for a driver to meet us there and take the car wherever we needed.

First, I went to the guest room where Joe's ex-wife, Samantha, was staying and knocked on the door. Samantha called out, "Is that you, Joe?"

I said, "No, sorry, it's Angelo."

She said, "Come in."

"How are you and Logan doing?"

"We're a little shaken up," Samantha said. "But Lewis's staff is taking great care of us. Do you have any news about Joe?"

"I'm sorry, not just yet, but I will soon. I've gotta go, but I'll check in with you with any updates."

Next, we went in the room that Vanesa had stayed in. We looked through anything for clues as to where she might be. We came up empty.

We then headed to Vanesa's safe house. It had been cleared by the police for us to enter. On the way, Grady and I discussed the files that Tanner had accumulated on the detectives. After just a few files, Grady asked, "How have these guys not been arrested?"

I said, "Tanner had to build a case. He was on the inside working undercover for Internal Affairs and got in with their unit. Right when they were presenting the case to the prosecutor, the mayor shut the case down."

Just then, my phone rang. It was Keith. I answered, "Hey, Keith, how's it—"

He cut me off, "Sorry, Angelo, but Vanesa turned on her computer. She's at Fibayson. I'll keep tracking as long as the computer is on, but I would hurry if I were you. I'll call if anything changes."

I tapped the driver and said, "Change of plan. We need to head to Fibayson's headquarters in the city."

He nodded, found the address, and quickly adjusted course to head in that direction. Grady said, "What's going on, Angelo?"

"Vanesa is at Fibayson. Keith tracked her computer. We need to get there, find her, and follow her when she leaves. Hopefully she will lead us to Joe."

"You've been tracking her computer?" Grady asked.

"We've been waiting for her to turn it on. Keith is a genius and knows how to get into anything. So, when she finally turned it on, he was able to use a geolocator and get her location."

"Let's go find your brother," Grady said.

▪ ▪ ▪

Fibayson's headquarters is in the financial district of New York City, set right on the waterfront. If you head toward the

Williamsburg Bridge, you will find a sprawling production facility for Fibayson that spans both sides of the bridge. They also have four research facilities throughout the city.

When we reached the headquarters, I called Keith. He confirmed that her computer was still on and that the computer was still there. We had also arranged for Lewis to send another car to Fibayson so we wouldn't miss Vanesa when she left. I stayed out in front of the building watching the main entrance in case she was on foot or caught a taxi. Luckily, there was a separate elevator bank to go to garage parking. Grady was stationed in that elevator lobby in case she had a car.

We had gotten set up just in time, because after just ten minutes, I spotted Vanesa coming out of the front entrance. She looked like she hadn't slept in days, with bags under her blue eyes and her hair a mess. Her head on a swivel, her eyes darted around as she headed for the taxi queue. I told the driver, "Follow that taxi!"

CHAPTER 66

MY EYES WERE GLUED to the taxi Vanesa was in. I told the driver to get closer, turn here, turn there. Eventually he said, "Mr. Barsotti, I've got this."

I finally sat back and called Lewis to update him. He said they were closing in on Waverly. He was the only detective with a family and therefore had the most to lose. I told him I'd call him once we got Joe back.

The taxi headed back uptown toward Lewis's building. When we were just two blocks from the VU, the taxi turned off and pulled up to the Marcel at Gramercy. Vanesa got out and ran inside. My driver pulled up and let me out. I waited for Grady to catch up.

When Grady got there, he strode up to the front desk, pulled out his badge, and asked for Vanesa Galloway's room. The clerk at the desk didn't know what to do, so he went and got a manager. When the manager came out, he said, "I'm sorry, guys, but I cannot release that information without a warrant."

Grady held up his badge again and said, "This involves a kidnapping, and the kidnapper is holding a man in one of your rooms. Would you like a whole raid here? Because I can arrange that. Or you can just give us what we need, and maybe only one door will be broken."

The manager started typing. "I'm sorry, but we don't have anyone by that name."

I said, "Check for Carter Galloway."

The manager started typing again. "No, no one by that name either."

I had an idea. I asked, "What about a Fibayson rate? They're only four miles away; do you have a special rate for them?"

The manager said, "Yes, but…hold on. I can look up anyone checked in using the Fibayson rate code." He started typing again then looked up from the screen and said, "I have five people currently in the hotel under the Fibayson rate."

He turned the computer around and showed us the list. Number four on the list was Lucy Barsotti. I stumbled back a step. Grady looked at me with bewilderment and said, "That's your late wife, right?"

I just nodded my head. Grady asked the manager for the room number of Lucy Barsotti. Room 1201. The manager pointed to the elevators and said, "Floor twelve, right when you walk off the elevator."

We headed up, listening to the cheery elevator music, but it didn't calm me at all. I was thinking about what the first thing I would say to Vanesa would be. *Is Joe here in the hotel room? Can we end this peacefully?*

When the doors opened, we noticed the hallway was clear. I let Grady take the lead. I wanted to just bust through the door and get my brother, but Grady knew how to handle these situations better. He put his hand over the peephole and knocked. Nothing. He tried again. Still no movement. He nodded to me. I lined up with the door, ready to kick it in, when the door opened.

Vanesa was standing there, gun in hand but not pointed at us. She waved us in and shut the door behind us. She said, "I just want this to be over. They killed my brother, and Fibayson has told me that they are done with me, that my part is done with. That I am no longer needed. They used me."

Surveying her appearance, I realized she wasn't the same person I'd met in the jail lobby. She was beaten down and exhausted. She started again, "Your brother is in the bathroom, unharmed, but he is tied up. I was never going to hurt him, but I needed the leverage, or they would have killed me."

I pushed past her to retrieve Joe. Grady stayed with her, at the ready. He had his hand on his gun, but I didn't think he would need it.

When Joe turned his face up to me when I came in, I saw the relief cross over his features. I untied him and helped him to his feet. He stretched out, and then gave me a big bear hug. He said, "I love you, bro. I knew you would find me. I'm sorry I didn't listen to you."

"I love you too. Are you OK?"

He said, "Yes, just a little sore from being tied up for the last couple of days. But overall, she treated me alright."

"Good. I'm glad you're safe now. Let's go figure out how we can end this."

CHAPTER 67

I KNEW WE DIDN'T have much time. The dirty detectives would be closing in to tie up all loose ends, which included Joe, Lewis, and me. They were probably after Vanesa first though. I figured after all she had done to us, we would use her as bait.

We restrained her hands, which she said wasn't necessary, but we didn't care. We took her back to the hotel where Lewis and Tanner were. They both were relieved that we had Joe safely back and that we had taken Vanesa. Officially she was in Grady's custody for kidnapping, but he was bringing her back with us to finish this.

Before we went into the room, Joe said, "Can I use your phone, Angelo? I need to call Samantha and Logan and let them know I'm OK."

"No problem. They're both at Lewis's under full protection until this is over."

We took Vanesa into the room to give Joe a few minutes of privacy. When he did enter the room, Tanner shook Joe's hand and Lewis gave him a hug. I said, "So, where are we on Waverly?"

Lewis said, "We think we have what we need to get him to flip, but let's see what Miss Galloway has to say."

I addressed Vanesa, "We probably don't have a lot of time, but let's start at the beginning. How long have you been working for Fibayson?"

Vanesa sat up straight and determined, but the pained look on her face told a different story. "They started threatening me when Lucy came to me. I am a legitimate lawyer, and I was working with your wife, Angelo. They told me that the case needed to go away or they would handle that for me. I have dealt with threats before; usually they are unsubstantiated. I just pushed forward like I always do. Then Lucy was killed. And then my brother Julian was killed in a 'car accident.' They called again and said to make the case go away. I did what they asked. I filed to have the class action thrown out due to insufficient evidence, and it was. They left me alone after that.

"Then I was put on the Craig Mazer case. I was just supposed to be working on background, helping Mr. Touré. Then I received another phone call. Somehow, they knew you were involved and wanted me to get close to you, Angelo, and see if you were still seeking justice for your wife. I said no, but then Mr. Touré called me into the case anyway. I'm not sure if they got to him as well or if it was a coincidence.

"When I met you and Lewis that first day, I knew I couldn't do it and that's why I ran. But they caught up to me, even with Lewis's guys watching. They told me that my brother was also on their payroll but wouldn't be much longer if I didn't come back and make sure you didn't find out any of this. I took that as a threat to my brother's life.

"That is where the dirty detectives come in. They are on Fibayson's payroll, but through the mayor's office via my brother, Carter Maxwell. They're the ones doing all the grunt work and making things disappear or blow up.

"Fibayson is running everything and making all the payments, but none of it will trace back to them. They have kept their hands completely clean. The only thing to do now is to at least stop the operation they have going now."

I gazed at her with budding sympathy but asked, "Why work behind our backs? We could have helped you. Protected you. Instead, you deceived us and fed information to the people responsible for my wife's death."

"No, I never fed them information. I just told them what they wanted to hear and that I had you and Lewis under control. That you would never find out the truth. I protected you."

CHAPTER 68

WE STEPPED INTO THE hall to discuss our options. Joe stayed in the room watching Vanesa, their roles now reversed. Lewis spoke first, "Angelo, this is up to you. We have Joe, but there are still dangerous people after us and Vanesa."

"No, this is Grady's call," I said.

Grady, pity in his eyes, said, "Angelo, I will follow your lead. This is your investigation. I'll take Vanesa in for the kidnapping charge, but only when you're done with her. I'm assuming you are going to use her to get to the detectives. I also need concrete evidence on the detectives; they are responsible for the bombings, but I need proof. I can use all the other evidence against them in trials to get their sentences extended. That's the only way we all win in this."

"What about Fibayson?" I asked. "They are the entity responsible for all of this!"

Tanner and Grady both shook their heads. Tanner said, "Vanesa said that they've kept their hands clean. I think we need to focus on the detectives and the mayor for now. And even the mayor may be untouchable. We don't know if he has been involved at all."

I begrudgingly say, "Fine, but if there's even a chance to get to them, we will. Agreed?"

They all agreed, and we headed back into the room. I asked Tanner and Grady to question Vanesa about the detectives. I wanted them to find out how much she knew and to get as much information as possible. I still couldn't believe what she had done, and I couldn't look her in the eyes.

Tanner started by saying, "Vanesa, you know that I know these guys. I worked within their group on the force. What can you tell us about them?"

"Well, I knew about Hank Dupont before we even called Dana at Precision. I knew what we would find; that's why I had us go to her. The detectives were hoping this would all be pinned on him, and it would end there. But Angelo, you called Grady, and the FBI took him in. I didn't think that's how it would go down. They couldn't let him talk, so they bombed the holding cells."

Grady interrupted Vanesa and said, "So you know that they did the bombing? The detectives themselves? And can you prove it? Also, how did they know the layout of the building?"

Vanesa thought before she answered. "I can't be one hundred percent sure, but they usually do the dirty work themselves. I'm sure Tanner would agree with that."

Tanner nodded.

Vanesa continued, "The only way I can prove it is to take you to their safe house. The storage unit was only used for storing money. The safe house has everything else. As for knowing the layout of the building, Fibayson has power in this city and worldwide. I'm guessing someone inside the FBI field office is on the payroll. Or maybe even someone higher up. Probably both."

I asked urgently, "Where is the safe house? We need to move now!"

"I'd have to take you there. I don't have an address."

CHAPTER 69

VANESA LED US BACK near the warehouses under the Brooklyn Bridge. She told us where to turn and, when we finally reached the building, where to park to be undetected. Keith directed us to get a scrambling device. It would knock out all the cameras' signals, but it would also knock out our phones. So, we also brought walkie-talkies, old school, to communicate.

Vanesa took us to a side door and told us that through the door would be a staircase and to go down it. We tread cautiously down the staircase to avoid making any noises. When we reached the basement, we could hear voices in the distance. They were saying something about all the cameras being out. And they'd also noticed that they didn't have any cell service either.

We split into pairs. Lewis and I went to the right, while Tanner and Grady went to the left. We'd left Vanesa, in restraints, with one of Lewis's guards. They would stay at the bottom of the stairs, his guard ready to catch any runners.

Lewis and I were the first to enter the room. It looked like an evidence locker. There were guns stacked on shelves, drugs stacked and categorized, and bombs. Lots and lots of bombs. Grims and Waverly whipped around in their chairs when they heard us, but we already had guns drawn and aimed at them. I demanded, "Where are the other two, Domingo and Chance?"

Grims, who looked like a boulder with feet, smiled and said, "Wouldn't you like to know?"

Grady and Tanner came around from the other side, and Grady said, "Yes, we would. And now!"

Grims paid him no mind, flippantly saying, "Looky what we have here. If it isn't Detective Rat. Don't you have some other cops to turn in?"

Tanner said, "Nope. All I care about is getting you and your band of cronies off the streets."

Grady hit the alert button on the walkie-talkies, and soon a team of FBI agents rushed into the room. We'd had them on standby as well as the FBI's bomb squad. Grady said, "We are taking you two in under the suspicion of bombing a federal facility. You can either tell us now where the other two are or you can also be charged with obstructing a federal investigation."

Grims just kept smirking and didn't say a word as the cuffs were put on him. Waverly stayed silent as well, but he wasn't acting as smug. When Grady's men started taking them out, I said, "Grady, let's split them up and leave Waverly here. I'd like to chat with him."

Grady nodded and took Grims out of the room. Tanner approached Waverly and asked, "Is this how you want to end your career? You want to leave your children fatherless? Your wife doesn't even have a job. How will she support your family? If you work with the FBI though, maybe, just maybe, you can salvage at least some of your family's life."

CHAPTER 70

WAVERLY BROKE QUICKLY. HE said that Domingo and Chance were on the mayor's security team. They took bombs to make sure Mayor Daniels' press conference to address the drug problems with Fibayson's new drug never happened. It was scheduled to be at New York Presbyterian Hospital, where many New York patients experiencing adverse effects of the drug were being treated. We had three hours before the mayor was scheduled to leave.

We decided to try to get to the mayor before he left but without calling it in. It was a tactical decision that Grady agreed with so that we didn't alert Domingo and Chance to the fact that we had figured out their plan. If it came down to it, we would lose those two and stop the caravan to avoid the bomb going off. But we needed to try and catch them first if we could.

The FBI took Vanesa, Grims, and Waverly to the field office to await questioning. Grady, Lewis, and I headed straight for city hall. We also had a couple members of the FBI bomb squad following behind us while the rest stayed at the safe house safely removing the bombs there. Tanner also stayed behind to inventory everything in the safe house. He would then go with the FBI and collect all the funds from the storage unit.

When we reached city hall, we still had two hours before the mayor was scheduled to leave. Lewis and I stayed in the garage while Grady, who was in plain clothes and shouldn't be recognized by Domingo and Chance, went inside. We were in his ear though, allowing us to communicate with him. We told him to head up to the floor the mayor was on and talk to Graham. We told him that Graham was the mayor's assistant, and he wouldn't get anywhere without him.

A little while after he'd gone in, Grady told us he'd discreetly flashed his badge a few times to gain entry and was now on his way to Graham's desk. We heard the exchange:

"Graham, I am Agent Humble with the New York FBI field office. I need to talk to the mayor, but it needs to be done quietly. Here are my credentials. Can you help make this happen?"

"I would like to help you, Agent Humble, but the mayor is already down at the Presbyterian Hospital. Before his press conference, he was meeting with those affected by the Fibayson drug."

"OK, can you get ahold of him?"

"Not directly, but I can get ahold of a member of his security detail. Would you like me to call him?"

"No, no. Who would you be calling? Who is in charge of the detail?"

"That would be Detective Domingo. I can call him right away if you need me to."

"Please don't do that. Thank you for your help. I'll just head down there and find the mayor myself. Do not call Detective Domingo. Understand?"

"Understood."

"Guys, pick me up in front of city hall. We need to move. We'll only have about an hour before the press conference, and we need to get to the mayor before that."

I said, "Loud and clear. Meet you in the front."

CHAPTER 71

WHEN WE ARRIVED AT the Presbyterian Hospital, we noticed a media circus gathered near a stage set up in front of the hospital and a crowd of supporters and opposers. We went around the back to the dock area. With Grady and his badge again, we went right through.

We located the reception desk, and I asked, "Where is the mayor visiting patients?"

Without glancing up, she answered that she could not give out that information. I nodded at Grady, who flashed his credentials again. After barely glimpsing the badge, she said, "Fifth floor, south wing. Elevators are right over there."

We split into three teams. Grady, Lewis, and I took the first elevator that came. A team of FBI agents grabbed the next elevator, while another set of FBI agents took the stairs. We waited for the team on the other elevator and then headed toward the reception desk on the south wing's fifth floor.

When the nurse stationed at the desk looked up, she did a double take at all the agents in full combat gear. She quietly asked, "Can I help you all?"

Grady said, "We need to know where the mayor is, now!"

She pointed to the hallway, but as we turned that way, I locked eyes with Domingo. He grabbed the mayor and fired shots at the rest of the protection detail, including Detective Chance. People began screaming and running in all directions. Domingo pulled the mayor into one of the patients' rooms. He was trapped, but he had hostages.

We could hear Mayor Daniels yelling, "You're supposed to be protecting me! Not pointing a gun at my head! What is wrong with you?"

The FBI team formed a semicircle around the outside of the room, while Grady and Lewis started getting people off the floor. I approached the FBI agents and said, "Can I try talking to him?"

They looked for Grady's instruction, but he was busy. Eventually, the lead man nodded and opened a space in the circle for me to get close. I said, "Domingo, it's over. No more people need to get hurt. We know that you and your detectives are working for Fibayson. They are the ones responsible for this. Don't continue making bad choices because of them."

It took about a minute or two—but felt like an eternity—before Domingo finally answered, "You don't know what you're up against here, Barsotti. If I had my choice, you and Pollard would have been taken out long ago. You know Vanesa was in charge of this. She is the main contact from Fibayson. We just work through her."

I said, "I know. But Fibayson has cut any ties to her, told her to kick rocks. They don't have any loyalty to you or your men. They will leave you hanging out for all of this."

Out of my peripheral vision, I saw Grady taking Detective Chance to get help for his bullet wound. I said, "Detective

Chance is still alive, and that's good for you. But I need you to release the mayor and come into custody with the FBI."

"I can't do that, Barsotti. They'll come after me, even if I'm in jail," Domingo said. "I know too much."

"Yes, but if you don't, these men out here are armed and ready to shoot you the first chance they get. You are backed into a corner with no escape. The best thing you can do is to cooperate."

No answer.

Suddenly, a single gunshot rang out, and the FBI agents pushed past me into the room.

CHAPTER 72

MAYOR DANIELS AND THE patient who had been in the room walked out visibly shaken. I walked into the room and immediately wished I hadn't. Domingo had been so afraid of what would happen to him, he took his life and any information with him. Fibayson was killing more than just the people taking their drugs.

I sought out Grady, who was grilling Detective Chance about where the bomb was. He kept denying that there was a bomb, and he didn't know what Grady was talking about.

I ran over to Mayor Daniels. I said, "I'm not sure of your involvement in all of this, but you cannot get into any of your vehicles in your caravan. Also, I need you to call down to any men in or near the vehicles and evacuate them."

He didn't question me, just did as I asked. Grady's two-person bomb squad got the location of the vehicles from Mayor Daniels, and they went to look for any devices.

"Mayor Daniels," I said, "you will not be giving a press conference today. At least not here. If you want to go back to city hall, then you can do whatever you'd like. But I will need to talk to you soon."

"How am I supposed to get to city hall? You just shut down the use of my caravan."

"I'm sure you can get a ride. Or there's always Uber."

Lewis was still taking care of patients and helping the nurses to calm everyone down. I returned to Grady and said, "I hope you will allow us help with the interrogations."

Grady shook his head and said, "You know I can't do that. You can come and listen in again if you'd like, but I will share with you everything we find. That is the best I can do."

"Can I at least talk to Vanesa? I need to know why she did all of this. I need the full story."

"I'm sure I can make that happen. I'm taking this one to the field office to join his friends. Are you coming with me?"

I replied, "I think Lewis and I will help as much as we can here, and then we will come by. Do what you need to do, but save Vanesa for last please."

"Will do. And thanks for another assist. Hopefully I can get these guys to break and tell me everything."

Grady went with Detective Chance, who was handcuffed to a hospital bed to be treated and then would be released into FBI custody. He left two agents with us to help get the fifth wing back in order. While we were helping, the bomb squad came up to tell us that they had found devices under the press conference podium, although the vehicles did not contain any bombs. They were able to disarm them and found no other devices around the press conference area. They were heading back to the warehouse to help finish up there and that the agents would need to go with them.

We stayed a couple more hours until the nurses basically told us to leave. They were very appreciative of the help, but they had had enough excitement for one day. We called Grady, and he said that they wouldn't start interrogations until the next day. So, I called Joe, and the three of us went to McGinty's for a well-deserved drink, some food, and fellowship.

CHAPTER 73

THE NEXT DAY, LEWIS, Joe, Tanner, and I went to the New York FBI field office. We were in the same room with the same equipment used during the Craig Mazer case. Each interview room had a camera, and we had a monitor and live feed to each one. We could see Detective Chance, Detective Waverly, Detective Grims, and Vanesa each seated, handcuffed to the table, and with some type of legal representation seated next to them. I wasn't surprised to see that Mr. Touré was there to represent Vanesa. The detectives each had their own appointed representative from the union.

Grady started with the detectives. Each of their stories were the same. All their answers pointed to Detective Domingo, a man who could not defend himself. They said he was in charge, he forced them to do it, and they had no other information. Grady went even harder on Waverly thinking that we had broken him once, maybe he could do it again. Not this time though. Somehow, they were all on the same page, with nothing differing in their scripts.

Then came Vanesa's interrogation. We had all been waiting for this moment. But it went as I had expected. Mr. Touré had instructed Vanesa to say no comment to every question Grady asked. Grady got fed up and left the room. He came down to where we were and asked, "Angelo, you want that chat now?"

I stood up and nodded my head solemnly. He led me to the interrogation room, and we walked in together. He said, "Mr. Touré, Mr. Barsotti would like to talk to your client. Off the record. If you agree, I will switch off the cameras, and you and I can wait outside."

He looked at Vanesa, who nodded her consent. As Mr. Touré stepped out, he gave me a pat on the back and whispered, "I'm sorry."

After Grady unhooked the cameras and left the room, I slumped down in the seat across from Vanesa and threw my hands in the air. Staring at her, I cried out, "Why? Just why?"

In a very quiet, subdued voice, she said, "Would you like the short version or the long version?"

"I think I deserve both!"

"Fine, short version…to protect my family."

"And the long version?"

"Fine," she agreed. "Can I start at the beginning?"

"Please do."

Vanesa closed her eyes and began, "It started when Lucy came to me with her findings and how the company disregarded her claims. She said she warned them and then people started dying. She wouldn't let it go. 'They have to pay!' is what she said.

"Her case was compelling, and she had all the facts I needed. It was an easy class action to win. Until it wasn't. As soon as I filed, I received a phone call from someone saying that they were from Fibayson, and it would be in my best interest to drop the case. I had been threatened before, so I didn't listen, like I told you before.

"But then Byron Mitchell, the president of Fibayson, came to my home. He brought files showing me everyone in my life whom I loved and cared for. He also had a whole binder full of incriminating files on my brother Carter. He apparently had been working with Fibayson since he became a campaign manager. They funded all his candidates if they toed the line on pharmaceutical policies. He also showed me pictures of someone cutting Julian's brakes because I didn't listen to them right away. They'd killed one brother already.

"Eventually, I cracked. I'm so sorry, Angelo. It was my entire family or Lucy, and I chose my family! The next day, Lucy was dead. I had to drop the case because she was the only witness and had all the files. They had won, and I thought it was over.

"Then the Craig Mazer case came to my firm. Once Grant Dogon was involved, they made me get involved as well. They said that Grant is a big supporter of theirs, and it would be in my best interest to get Craig off the murder charge.

"When I met you, I told myself that before the case was over, I would tell you what had happened to Lucy. That's why I gave you the note. As soon as I gave it to you, though, I got scared and ran. I was responsible for her death. Not directly, but I made choices that made it so. I still had to get Craig Mazer out of jail, and luckily, you did that for me. But I couldn't come back.

"Then finally, my brother called me and said that four detectives had paid him a visit. They beat the hell out of him and eventually told him that if I didn't come back to clean up the mess I started, then he would be killed. The mess was you starting to poke around into Lucy's death.

"I came back to push you in other directions, hoping you would give up. But when I got back here, I could tell that you would never give up. The detectives wanted to just take you and Lewis out. They said that it would end it all right then. I told them that would only bring more questions, and they may never escape the scrutiny. If you haven't figured this out yet, the detectives were at your house the night of Lucy's murder. They get paid through intermediaries from Fibayson to clean up, hide evidence, and produce reports that conceal the truth.

"So, I brought in Camila and coached her on what to say, so you would believe I had a new case. It was all a smoke screen. Just like the fires, they were there to distract and make you look in other directions. They only burned up old equipment and files that were of no use to them anymore and made it look like key things were being destroyed. Oh, and Nathan Grimble, he was in on it too. He passed the fires to the police because the detectives threatened him. But then he grew a conscience and started claiming arson. So, the detectives did what they do and made him disappear.

"All of that led me to a desperate attempt to make you stop looking."

I said, "You kidnapped my brother."

"I kidnapped your brother. You saw what they did to Lewis's men at my safe house and Camila's safe house. I couldn't let that go on anymore. I just needed you to stop. I figured that it had worked on me, protecting my family at all costs, that maybe it would work on you too. But then they killed my other brother, and I was done. Done running, done doing Fibayson's bidding, done."

Done myself, I stood up abruptly and left the room. I didn't look back; I didn't say goodbye. She didn't deserve it. She made her choices, and I made mine. A clean break.

EPILOGUE

WITHOUT DETECTIVE DOMINGO, AGENT Grady couldn't pin the bombing of the federal building on the other detectives. But Tanner was able to reopen the Internal Affairs case against them and add the murder of Carter Maxwell/Galloway and the attempted murder of Mayor Daniels. The three dirty detectives would spend the rest of their lives in jail.

It was discovered that Carter Maxwell had used the mayor's office to call into the police department to shut down the Internal Affairs investigation. Grady and I interviewed the mayor after Carter's death. Although he wasn't a suspect in the murder, we were trying to gauge what he knew of Carter's actions with Fibayson. He said he had no clue about any of it, and he was at the hospital to denounce the practices of Fibayson and reject any further donations from them. After the rest of the FBI investigation, Mayor Daniels was cleared of any involvement.

Vanesa was sent to jail for 25 years for kidnapping and obstruction of justice.

■ ■ ■

Internal Affairs Officer Tanner walked into his superior's office. His commander said, "Nice work on getting those detectives nailed. I know it took longer than expected, but you did well. You also got the corruption rate in the New York PD reduced by fifty percent in the last quarter with your arrests."

"Thank you, sir. That's my job, and I take it seriously."

His commander leaned in close. "So, I have one other question for you. I know you worked closely with Angelo Barsotti. I need to know… Does he have any inclination that his wife is still alive?"

"No, sir. He believes at this point that he has solved her murder. He doesn't even have an inkling that she could be alive."

"OK, good. I knew I chose the right person for this case."

ACKNOWLEDGMENTS

I FIRST WANT TO thank my wife, Dawn, because without her this still wouldn't have been possible. Next, I want to thank my kids for their continued help selling my first book because they love me so much. Then I want to thank my mother and father for their unbelievable support for this writing endeavor, my biggest social supporters as well. And lastly, I'd like to thank all the people who helped me get this book to the level that I wanted it to be: Milade Rasooli, my day one reader; Karen Tucker, my editor; Beth Lamkemeyer, my ever supportive friend; E Lavaniel Jr. S, my plot buddy; Joni Erikson, my ongoing English teacher; Peggy Nehmen, awesome book designer; Steve Torretta and Stacey Lampe, my friendly editors; and Marge Leuthen, my proofreader.

ABOUT THE AUTHOR

RYAN SPELL IS FROM St. Louis, Mo., where he still resides. He is an environmental consultant by trade but has always read great fiction books. He decided long ago to write his own, and he finally did. *A Pharmacy of Lies* is his second book. Ryan has a wife and two children, both boys.

FROM THE AUTHOR

THANK YOU FOR READING *A Pharmacy of Lies.* If you enjoyed this book (or even if you didn't), please visit the site where you purchased it and write a brief review. Your feedback is important to me and will help other readers decide whether to read the book, too. I hope if anything else, you will continue reading books, from me or any other author. Writing should inspire reading.

If you'd like to get notifications of new releases and special offers on my books, please join my email list by signing up on my website, www.ryanspell.com.

Ryan Spell, 2024